STAR TREK 2

CIRCLING THE SOLAR SPHERE
IN SEARCH OF NEW WORLDS
AND HIGH ADVENTURE

CAPTAIN JAMES KIRK—Assigned to
the top position in Space Service—
Starship Command—Kirk alone must
make decisions in his contact with
other worlds that can affect the future
course of civilization throughout the
Universe.

SCIENCE OFFICER SPOCK—Inheriting
a precise, logical thinking pattern
from his father, a native of the planet
Vulcan, Mr. Spock maintains a dangerous Earth trait . . . an intense
curiosity about things of alien origin.

LT. UHURA—Easily the most popular
member of the crew, the truly "out-of-
this-world" female has drawn the important assignment of scan engineer
on her first mission in deep space.

WITH A CREW OF 400
SKILLED SPECIALISTS, THE
MAMMOTH SPACE SHIP
ENTERPRISE BLASTS OFF FOR
INTERGALACTIC INTRIGUE
IN THE UNEXPLORED REALMS
OF OUTER SPACE.

STAR
TREK
2

JAMES BLISH

Based on the Award-winning Television Series
Created by Gene Roddenberry

BANTAM BOOKS
TORONTO · NEW YORK · LONDON · SYDNEY

to my new-found relative
BARBARA BESADNY
and all the other
"Star Trek" fans
who wrote to me about the first book

RL 8, IL 8-up

STAR TREK 2
A Bantam Book | February 1968
24 printings through December 1979

25th printing

ISBN 0–553–13877–4

Published simultaneously in the United States and Canada

PRINTED IN THE UNITED STATES OF AMERICA

CONTENTS

ARENA
(Gene L. Coon)

Captain James Kirk of the USS *Enterprise* was the absolute master of the largest and most modern vessel in the Starfleet Service, of all the complex apparatus and weaponry aboard her, and of the manifold talents of 430 highly trained crewmen.

And at the moment, he was stranded on a nearly barren artificial asteroid, location unknown, facing a tyrannosaurlike creature whose survival depended upon its killing Kirk, and equipped with absolutely nothing except a small translator-recorder useless as a weapon.

The situation had developed with bewildering rapidity. Originally, the *Enterprise* had received a call from the Earth outpost on Cestus Three, part of a planetary system on the very edge of an unexplored quadrant of the galaxy. The base commandant, an old soldier named Travers, had asked Kirk to beam down with the tactical staff of the *Enterprise;* and since things were quiet in this sector of space and Travers was famous in the Service for setting a good table, all six men had accepted cheerfully.

But the invitation had been a trap—a prerecorded trap. They had found the settlement in smoking ruins, the personnel dead. Furthermore, within minutes after its arrival the landing party was also under attack—and so was the *Enterprise.*

Evidently, the enemy, whoever he was, did not have the transporter and had no idea of its capabilities; after five minutes' inconclusive exchange of shots, the landing party was whisked away clean. The enemy ship broke off the engagement and fled, at fantastically high acceleration.

Kirk had no intention of letting it get away, however. It seemed obvious that any attempt to ambush the *Enterprise's* tactical staff and captain, and then to destroy the starship itself, could only be a prelude to a full-scale invasion. Furthermore, the unknown enemy was well armed —the damage its ship had suffered thus far had been minor, despite its flight—and peculiarly ruthless, as witness its having wiped out 512 helpless people at an inoffensive scientific outpost simply to bait its trap. As Science Officer Spock had pointed out, that ship could not be allowed to reach its home base; presumably, as long as that unknown world was kept in the dark about Federation strength, it would hold off its next attack—thus buying precious time for a defense buildup.

The enemy seemed equally anxious to avoid leading the *Enterprise* to its home planet. It took complex evasive action, again at incredibly high speed; the *Enterprise* had difficulty in closing with her even at warp eight, two factors above maximum safe speed.

And then, suddenly, everything stopped.

It was absolutely impossible, but it happened. At one moment, both vessels were flashing through subspace at over a hundred times the speed of light—and in the next, both were floating in normal space, motionless relative to a small, nearby solar system, engines inoperative, all weapons dead.

"Report!" Kirk snapped.

But there was no damage, nothing abnormal—except that the *Enterprise* could neither move nor fight, nor, apparently, could the enemy.

"We're being scanned, sir," Communications Officer Uhura said.

"From the alien ship?"

"No, sir," she said. "From that solar system ahead. Nothing hostile—no tractors or weapon sensors, just scanners."

"Stopping us like this might be considered hostile," Kirk said drily.

"Getting something else, Captain—a modulation of the main frequency . . ."

Abruptly, the lights dimmed and there was a low hum from the main viewing screen. The starry scene from outside promptly dissolved into a twisting, confused mass of color and lines. At the same time a humanoid voice, strong and yet somehow youthful, shook the air of the bridge. The voice said:

"We are the Metrons."

Kirk and Spock exchanged speculative glances. Then

the Science Officer said, quite composedly: "How do you do?"

The voice's owner paid no apparent attention. It continued:

"You are one of two craft that have come into our space on a mission of violence. This is not permissible. Our analysis further shows that your violent tendencies are inherent. Hence we will resolve your conflict in the way most suited to your natures. Captain James Kirk!"

"This is Captain Kirk," Kirk said, after a moment's hesitation.

"We have prepared a planetoid with a suitable atmosphere, temperature and gravity. You will be taken there, as will the captain of the Gorn ship that you have been pursuing. You and your opponent will be provided with a translator-recorder. You can keep a record, or communicate with each other, should you feel the need. But not with your ships. You will each be totally alone, and will settle your dispute alone."

"Just what makes you think you can interfere . . ." Kirk began angrily.

"It is you who are doing the interfering. We are simply putting a stop to it—within your own violent frame of reference. The place we have prepared for you contains sufficient resources for either of you to construct weapons lethal to the other. The winner of the ordeal will be permitted to go on his way unharmed. The loser, along with his ship, will be destroyed in the interests of peace. The contest will be one of ingenuity against ingenuity, brute strength against brute strength. The outcome will be final."

With that, silently, the ship around Kirk vanished.

The first thing he saw was the Gorn. It was a biped, a reptile, a lizard that walked like a man. It stood about six feet four, with tremendous musculature, dully gleaming skin, a ridge of hard plate running down its back, and a strong, thick tail. The tail did not look prehensile; rather, it seemed to be a balancing organ, suggesting that the creature could run very fast indeed if it wished. The head was equipped with two tiny earholes and a wide mouth full of sharp teeth.

This, then, was the enemy, the raider, the destroyer of

Cestus Three. It was wearing a garment like a short robe, belted; at the belt hung a small electronic device. It wore no shoes; clawed feet dug deeply into the ground, indicating considerable weight. Shooting a wary glance down at himself, Kirk discovered that his own clothing and equipment were identical.

Kirk and the Gorn stared at each other. All around them was a rocky, barren terrain, with a peculiar gray-green sky and occasional clumps of vegetation, some of it fairly tall, but none of it familiar. The air was cold and dry.

Kirk wondered if the Gorn was as uncomfortable as he was. Probably, but for different reasons. The meddling Metrons would surely have allowed neither of them an advantage in environment; after all, this planetoid was artificial—deliberately constructed to be an arena for a trial of champions, and for nothing else.

The Gorn moved. It was closing in on Kirk. It looked quite capable of killing him with its bare hands. Kirk moved sidewise, warily.

The Gorn did not appear to want to take any chances. As it too circled, it passed close to a gnarled object like a small tree, perhaps eight to ten inches through the trunk, and about ten feet high. With a quick look at Kirk, the Gorn hissed softly, reached out, and broke off a thick branch. The move seemed to cost it very little effort, whereas Kirk doubted that he could have done it at all.

Then, suddenly, holding the branch aloft like a club, the Gorn was charging him.

Kirk sprang aside barely in time. As the Gorn passed, somewhat off-balance, Kirk swung a killing blow into its midriff. The impact nearly broke his hand, but it seemed to have no other effect. The club lashed back, knocking Kirk sprawling against the rocks.

The Gorn wheeled around, clumsily but swiftly, and pounced. Kirk, dazed, tried to counter with a forearm blow to the throat, but it was like hitting an elephant. Then the creature was gripping him like a grizzly. Kirk's arm just managed to keep the teeth away, but that grip was going to break his back.

Freeing his arms with a sudden twist, Kirk boxed the Gorn's earholes with cupped hands. The Gorn screamed and staggered back, shaking its huge head. Springing to his feet, Kirk picked up a boulder as big as his head and hurled it at the Gorn with all his strength.

It struck the Gorn fair on the chest. The creature lurched slightly, but it did not seem to be hurt. Hissing shrilly, it bent to pick up a boulder of its own. The thing must have weighed a thousand pounds, but the Gorn got it aloft in one titanic jerk.

Kirk ran.

The rock hit behind him with an explosive crack, and flying splinters cut into the calf of one leg like shrapnel. Still hobbling as fast as he could, Kirk looked back over his shoulder.

The Gorn was not following. Instead, it was heaving up another rock. Then, as if realizing that Kirk was now out of range, it let the huge mass drop. It seemed to be grinning, although as far as Kirk had been able to see, it never wore any other expression.

Kirk looked around, panting. He seemed to be in a gully, though there was no sign that water had ever run in it—after all, there hadn't even been such a planet many hours ago. There were rocks everywhere, some of them brilliantly colored, and an occasional outcropping of quartzlike crystals. Here and there were patches of scrubby, tough-looking brush, some of it resembling cacti, some mesquite, and even an occasional stand of a large, bamboolike growth. There was nothing that looked as though it could possibly be converted into a weapon, no matter what the Metron had said.

Kirk sat down, rubbing his injured leg but taking great care to watch the now-distant Gorn, and looked over the device at his belt. It looked quite like a tricorder, but both smaller and simpler—though simpler, at least, it doubtless was not. Kirk turned it on with the obvious switch.

"Calling the *Enterprise*. Captain James Kirk calling the *Enterprise*."

For a moment, there was no answer. Then the instrument said, in good but rather stilted English:

"You forget, Captain. We cannot reach our ships. We are alone here, you and I—just one against the other."

He looked back the way he had come. Sure enough, the Gorn seemed to be speaking behind one raised hand.

Kirk had not, of course, forgotten that he had been

5

told he could not raise the *Enterprise;* he had simply wanted to test the statement. What he had forgotten was that the small instrument had been said to be a translator, as well as a recorder. He would have to be very careful not to mutter to himself after this.

After a moment, he said tentatively, "Look here, Gorn, this is insane. Can't we patch up some kind of truce?"

"Out of the question," the translator said promptly. "That would result only in our staying here until we starved. I cannot speak for you, but I see no water here, nor anything I could eat—with the possible exception of you."

"Neither do I," Kirk admitted.

"Then let us not waste time in sentimental hopes. The rules are what they are: One of us must kill the other."

Kirk hung the device back on his belt. The Gorn was right, and that was most definitely that.

He scrambled over to look at the bamboolike stuff. Each stalk was perhaps three to four inches in diameter —and, as he discovered by trying to break a section loose, it was as hard as iron. Hitting it with a rock even produced a distinctly metallic clank. Perhaps it picked up iron from the soil, as horsetails pick up calcium oxalate, or some prairie grasses pick up selenium. Useless.

He moved on up the gully, which got steadily deeper; he lost sight of the Gorn almost at once. Well, the risk had to be taken; staying where he was had gotten him nowhere.

Earthen banks, rather like bluish clay, reared on both sides of him now. One was steep, but the slope of the other was gentle enough to permit him to clamber up it if he had to.

Sticking out of the clay were the pyramidal points of a number of large crystals. Hopefully, Kirk pried one of them out. It was about the size of a hen's egg, and glittered brilliantly even under this sunless sky. The shape and the brilliancy were unmistakable: It was a diamond, and one that would have made the Kohinoor look like a mail-order zircon. And not only were there more of them imbedded in the clay, but the floor of the gully, he now saw, was a litter of them, in all sizes down to fine sand.

An incredible fortune—and again, utterly useless. None of the gems was sharp enough to be used as a weapon point, and he had no way to cut them. Their only use was to show that this planet was indeed an artificial construction—but Kirk had never doubted that, anyhow. He would have traded the whole wealth of them for a hand phaser, or even a medieval crossbow and a quiver of bolts for it.

The gully turned just ahead. Throwing the diamond away, Kirk went around the bend. The Metron had said that there were the raw materials of weapons here somewhere, if only he—

At the next step, his ankle struck a taut vine, and he went sprawling. At the same moment there was a sharp *crack!* as of wood splitting, and then one whole side of the gully seemed to be roaring down upon him.

He rolled frantically in the other direction, but not fast enough to prevent one rock from slamming into his chest. He felt a rib break. Staggering to his feet, he ran for the nearest cover, a sculptured overhang almost deep enough in back to be called a cave. There he stopped, breathing hard and nursing his rib cage—his whole body seemed to be one enormous bruise—and inspected the snare that had almost killed him through the gradually settling dust.

It was very simple and highly ingenious: a length of stretched vine to serve as a trigger, a broken branch, a heap of carefully stacked boulders that had been freed when the branch had been pulled loose.

Above him, Kirk heard the tick of large claws on rock, and then a sharp hiss of what could only have been disappointment. Kirk grinned mirthlessly. It had been near enough. He peered cautiously out of his hole and upward, just in time to see the Gorn on the lip of the gully on the other side, moving away. The creature was carrying something long and shiny in one hand. Kirk could not tell exactly what it was, but the fact that the Gorn had a torn scrap of his tunic wrapped around that hand was clue enough. It was a daggerlike blade, evidently chipped out of obsidian glass.

Then the creature was gone, but Kirk did not feel the least bit reassured. So far, the Gorn was way ahead, not only on strength, but on ingenuity. First a snare—now a dagger.

Well, then, back to the Stone Age with a vengeance. If Kirk could find a flint point, another length of vine, a sufficiently long stick, he might make a spear. That would give him the advantage of reach against the Gorn's dagger. On the other hand, would a spear penetrate that hide? There was only one way to find out.

A sufficiently large chip of flint, however, obstinately failed to turn up. All that was visible on the floor of the overhang was a wash of brilliant yellow powder.

The stuff looked familiar, and on a hunch, Kirk picked up a small handful of it and breathed on it. It gave out the faint crackle characteristic of flowers of sulfur when moistened.

Kirk grimaced. What a maddening planet. Sand of high-purity sulfur, veritable beaches of diamonds, iron-concentrating bamboos; and at the back of the cave here, outcroppings of rocks covered with a yellowish-white effluvium, like saltpeter. The only way he could make any sort of weapon out of a mélange like that would be with a smelter and a forge—

Wait a minute. Just a minute, now. There was something at the back of his mind—something very ancient . . .

With a gulp of hope, he ran back toward the growth of bamboolike stuff.

With a sharp rock, he managed to break off about a three-foot length of one tube, at one of its joints. The tube was closed at one end, open at the other. Ideal.

Now, the diamonds. He took up only the smallest, the most sandlike, measuring them by handfuls into the tube. He could only hope that his memory of the proportions—seventy-five, fifteen, ten—was correct; in any event, he could only approximate the measures under these conditions. Now, one of the large egg-shaped diamonds; this he put into his mouth, since the tunic did not come equipped with pockets.

Back up the gully, down and around the bend to the overhang. Into the tube went sulfur, saltpeter. Covering the end, he shook the tube until a little of the mixture poured out into his palm showed an even color, though certainly not the color it should have been.

A stone point penetrated the bamboo at the base, though it was hard work. A bit of torn tunic for a patch, and ram it all home with a stick. Then the egg-shaped diamond; then another patch, and ram again. Finally, a piece of flint; it did not have to be large, not any more.

"Captain," the translator at his belt said. He did not answer.

"Captain, be reasonable," the translator said. "Hiding will do you no good. If it is a matter of competitive starvation, I think my endurance is greater than yours. Why not come out, and die like a warrior?"

Kirk ignored it. Shredding another piece of cloth from the tunic, he began to strike the piece of flint over it, using the translator—at last it had a use!—as the steel. Sparks flew, but the cloth would not catch. If it was noninflammable—

"You cannot destroy me," the translator said. "Let us be done with it. I shall be merciful and quick."

"Like you were at Cestus Three?" Kirk said.

"You were intruding," the translator said. "You established an outpost in our space. Naturally we destroyed it."

Kirk did not stop striking sparks, but he was at the same time thoughtful. What the Gorn said was perhaps reasonable, from its point of view. Very little was known about that arm of the galaxy; perhaps the Gorn had a right to regard it as theirs—and to be alarmed at the setting up of a base there, and by the advent of a ship the size of the *Enterprise*. Nevertheless . . .

Smoke rose from the shredded cloth. He raised it to his lips, blowing gently. It was catching.

"All right, Gorn," he told the translator. "Come and get me if you think you can. I'm under the overhang just past where you set your snare."

There was a sharp hiss, and then the clear sound of the Gorn's claws, coming at a run up the gully. Kirk had miscalculated. The creature was closer than he had thought —and faster. Frantically he struggled to align the clumsy bamboo tube.

The Gorn leapt into view, its obsidian knife raised. Kirk slapped the burning piece of clothes against the touchhole, and the makeshift cannon went off with a splintering roar. The concussion knocked Kirk down; the semicave was filled with acrid smoke.

He groped to his feet again. As the smoke cleared, he saw the Gorn, slumped against the other wall of the gully. The diamond egg had smashed its right shoulder; but it was bleeding from half a dozen other places too, where diamond chips had flown out of the cannon instead of igniting.

The knife lay between them. Leaping forward, Kirk snatched it up, hurled himself on the downed alien. The knife's point found one of the wounds.

"Now," Kirk said hoarsely, "now let's see how tough your hide is!"

The Gorn did not answer. Though conscious, it seemed to be in shock. It was all over. All Kirk had to do was shove.

He could not do it. He rose, slowly.

"No," he said. "We're in the same pickle. You're trying to save your ship, the same as I am. I won't kill you for that."

Suddenly furious, Kirk looked up at the greenish, overcast sky.

"Do you hear?" he shouted. "I won't kill him! You'll have to get your entertainment some place else!"

There was a long pause. Kirk stared down at the wounded alien; the Gorn stared back. Its translator had been shattered by the impact; it could not know what Kirk had said. But it did not seem to be afraid.

Then it vanished.

Kirk sat down, dejected and suddenly, utterly weary. Right or wrong, he had lost his opportunity now. The Metron had snatched the Gorn away.

Then there was a humming, much like that he had heard so long ago aboard ship, when the screen had been scrambled. He turned.

A figure was materializing under the overhang. It was not very formidable—certainly nothing so ominous, so awe-inspiring as its voice had suggested. Also, it was very beautiful. It looked like a boy of perhaps eighteen.

"You're a Metron," Kirk said listlessly.

"True," said the figure. "And you have surprised us, Captain."

"How?" Kirk said, not much interested. "By winning?"

"No. We had no preconceptions as to which of you would win. You surprised us by refusing to kill, although you had pursued the Gorn craft into our space with the intention of destroying it."

"That was different," Kirk said. "That was necessary."

"Perhaps it was. It is a new thought. Under the circumstances, it is only fair to tell you that we lied to you."

"In what way?"

"We said that the ship of the loser of this personal combat would be destroyed," said the Metron. "After all, it would be the winner—the stronger, the more resourceful race—who would pose the greatest threat to us. It was the winner we planned to destroy."

Kirk lurched to his feet. "Not my ship," he said dangerously.

"No, Captain. We have changed our minds. By sparing your helpless enemy—who would surely have killed you in like circumstances—you demonstrated the advanced trait of mercy. This we hardly expected—and it leaves us with no clear winner."

"What did you do with the Gorn, then?"

"We sent him back to his ship. And in your case, we misinterpreted your motives. You sincerely believed that you would be destroying the Gorn ship to keep the peace, not break it. If you like, we shall destroy it for you."

"No!" Kirk said hastily. "That's not necessary. It was a . . . a misunderstanding. Now that we've made contact, we'll be able to talk to the Gorn—reach an agreement."

"Very good," said the Metron. "Perhaps we too shall meet again—in a few thousand years. In any event, there is hope for you."

And abruptly, the *Enterprise* sprang into being around Kirk.

Turmoil broke out on the bridge. Ship's Surgeon McCoy was the first to reach Kirk's side.

"Jim! Are you all right?"

"To be quite honest with you," Kirk said dazedly, "I don't know. I just wish the world would stop popping in and out at me."

"I gather you won," Spock said. "How did you do it?"

"Yes . . . I guess so. I'm not quite sure. I thought I did it by reinventing gunpowder—with diamond dust for charcoal. But the Metrons say I won by being a sucker. I don't know which explanation is truer. All the Metrons would tell me is that we're a most promising species—as predators go."

"I could not have put the matter more neatly myself,"

Spock said. "But, Captain, I would be interested to know what it is you're talking about—when you feel ready, of course."

"Yes, indeed," Kirk said. "In the meantime, posts, everybody. It's time we got back down to business. And, Mr. Spock, about that explanation . . ."

"Yes, sir?"

"I suggest you raise the question again, in, say, a few thousand years."

"Yes, sir."

And the odd thing about Spock, the captain reflected, was that he *would* wait that long too, if only he could figure out a way to live through it—and when the time had all passed, Spock would remember to ask the question again.

Kirk hoped he would have an answer.

A TASTE OF ARMAGEDDON

(Robert Hamner and Gene L. Coon)

Ambassador Fox was something of a cross to Captain Kirk, and to most of his officers, for that matter. In addition to having a very high regard for his own importance —which is not necessarily a handicap in a man, provided he also has a sense of humor—he had a remarkably short temper for a career diplomat.

But the mission was his, and he had to be put up with. There was no question about the importance of that. Eminiar VII was by all accounts the most advanced planet of its star cluster, NGC 321, having had space flight for hundreds of years. Nevertheless, as of fifty years ago they had never ventured beyond their own solar system, and for a very good reason: They had been at war with their nearest neighbor. The vessel making the report, the USS *Valiant*, was listed as missing—presumably as a product of the hostilities. It was Fox's job to establish diplomatic relations with them.

It evidently was not going to be easy. At first contact with the *Enterprise*, Eminiar VII sent Code 710—a warning not to approach the planet under any circumstances. Kirk was more than willing to comply; after all, it *was* their planet, and he intensely disliked gunboat diplomacy. But Ambassador Fox insisted, and he had command power if he wanted to exercise it. He frequently did.

Kirk beamed down to the planet with Mr. Spock, Yeoman Manning and two security guards, leaving Scott, his engineer, in charge of the ship. In view of the warning, they all carried number-one phasers, in addition to a tricorder, of which Yeoman Manning was in charge.

But there was no overt hostility. They materialized in a corridor of a building that, judging by the traffic, was an official establishment of some kind, and were met solely by a very pretty girl who introduced herself as Mea Three and promptly offered to take them to the High Council. Her manner was cool, but correct.

13

The High Council proved to consist of four pleasant-looking men seated at a table in a large room that had in it also a faint hum of machinery, though none was evident. As Kirk and his party entered, all four rose and smiled.

"I am Anan Seven," said the one farthest to the left. "I am sorry to see you here. But you are here, and we must do everything possible to make you comfortable. Won't you sit down?"

"I'm Captain Kirk, James T. Kirk of the Starship *Enterprise,* representing the United Federation of Planets. This is my first officer, Mr. Spock. Lieutenant Galloway. Lieutenant Osborne. Yeoman Manning."

"Welcome to Eminiar," Anan said, making a formal little bow. Everyone sat, and there was a moment of silence as each party studied the other.

"Well, Captain," Anan said at last, "since you chose to disregard our warning, I suppose we must proceed to the business at hand. What can we do for you?"

"Our mission, sir, is to establish diplomatic relations between your people and mine. The Federation badly needs a treaty port in this cluster."

"Impossible, I'm afraid," Anan said.

"Oh? Would you mind telling me why?"

"Because of the war."

"You are *still* at war?" Kirk said.

"We have been at war," Anan said, "for five hundred years."

Kirk raised his eyebrows. "You conceal it well. Mr. Spock?"

"Sir," Spock said to Anan, "we have completely scanned your planet. We find it highly advanced, prosperous in a material sense, comfortable for your people—and completely peaceful. Seemingly an ideal, flourishing, highly civilized culture, which obviously should have ties with our Federation. There is no evidence of war whatsoever."

"Casualties among our civilian population," Anan said evenly, "total from one to three million dead each year, from direct enemy attack. This is why we warned you away, Captain. As long as your ship is orbiting this planet, it is in severe danger."

"With whom are you at war?" Spock said.

"Vendikar, the third planet in this system. Originally settled by our people, and as advanced as we are—and a ruthless enemy."

"Nevertheless . . ." Spock began. He got no further than that word. Suddenly the room was clamoring with a shrill, whooping siren. Anan, his face stern, stood instantly, pressing a button.

The result was astonishing. The siren stopped, but the entire rear wall of the Council room slid aside, revealing another room of the same size that harbored an installation of enormous intricacy. It was too big and too involved to take it all in at once; Kirk got a quick impression of a long bank of computers, a number of lighted graphs on the walls, a large illuminated grid that might have been a map.

"You will have to excuse us," Anan said. "We are in fact under attack at this moment. Mea, care for our guests."

All four of the council members took positions at the machinery, where several other operators were already at work. Kirk, baffled, looked first at Spock, who shrugged, and then at Mea.

"It will not last long," the girl said.

"Don't you take shelter?"

"There is no shelter, Captain."

"Are these attacks frequent?" Spock said.

"Oh, yes. But we retaliate promptly."

Beckoning to Spock, Kirk moved off into the newly revealed room—the war room, Kirk supposed. No attempt was made to stop them. At the large grid, an operator sat at a console. Flashes spattered over the grid, seemingly at random; at each flash, the operator pushed what was evidently a matching button. Kirk studied it, but it conveyed nothing to him; as he had expected, he could not read the mapping conventions of Eminiar. Beside him, however, Mea gasped suddenly.

"A hit!" she said. "A hit in the city!"

"Mr. Spock, hear any explosions?"

"None. Yeoman Manning, are you getting any radiation readings or any other kind of disturbance on the tricorder?"

"Not a thing."

Kirk turned to Mea. "If this is an attack," he said,

15

"would you mind telling me what weapons the enemy is using?"

"Fusion bombs," she said. "Materialized by transporter over the targets. They are very accurate. My parents were killed in the last attack."

Kirk flipped out his communicator and called the ship. "Mr. Scott, are you still scanning this planet's surface?"

"Of course, sir," Scott's voice said promptly. "Per your orders."

"Anything unusual?"

"Nothing, sir. All quiet."

As Kirk put the communicator away, something buzzed on the boards before them and one of the computers extruded a card from a slot. Anan took it and stared at it, his face grim. Then he handed it to the man next to him.

"Just as it happened fifty years ago, Sar," he said.

Sar nodded, his face sad. "We warned them."

"Alert a security detachment. They may be needed."

"Sir," Kirk said, "I have been in contact with my ship, which has this entire planet under surveillance. All the time this so-called attack has been in progress, we have been monitoring you. There has been no attack—no explosions, no radiation, no disturbances whatsoever. Now if this is just some sort of game . . ."

"It is not a game," Anan said. "Half a million people have just been killed."

"Entirely by computers," Spock said suddenly.

"That's quite correct," Anan said. "Their deaths are registered. They are then given twenty-four hours to report to the disintegration chambers. Since the immediate danger appears to be over, I can explain at somewhat greater length. You must understand, Captain, that no two planets could carry on an all-out nuclear war for five hundred years. Such a war would not last five hundred hours. We were forced to find another solution."

"In other words," Spock said, "Vendikar's attack was a theoretical one."

"On the contrary, it was quite real. It is simply launched mathematically. If it is successful, the casualties are computed, identified, and ordered to report for disposition. Theoretical? I lost my wife in the last attack. It is sometimes hard—but our civilization lives. The people die, but the culture goes on."

"Do you mean to tell me," Kirk said, "that your people just . . . walk into a disintegrator when they're told to?"

"They do. They are at war and they know it."

"I've heard of some cold-blooded arrangements," Kirk said, "but this one takes the prize."

"It is cold-blooded," Spock agreed. "But it does have a certain logic about it."

"I am glad you approve," Anan said.

"I do not approve," Spock said coldly. "I understand, which is something else entirely."

"Good," Anan said. "Then you will recall that we warned you not to come here. You chose to disregard my warning. Once in orbit around our planet, your ship became a legitimate target. It has been classified destroyed by an incoming missile."

He made a quick gesture. Kirk spun around. There were four very large uniformed men behind the *Enterprise* party. All four held unfamiliar but quite lethal-looking weapons.

"All persons aboard your ship have twenty-four hours to report to our disintegration chambers. To insure their cooperation, I am ordering you and your party held in custody against their surrender. The same thing, by the way, happened to your ship the *Valiant*, fifty years ago. Killed to the last man."

"You are not," Kirk said through his teeth, "going to harm my ship. Is that clear?"

"If possible, we shall spare the ship," Anan said. "But its passengers and crew are already dead. Put them in class-one detention."

"Class-one detention" proved to be comfortable—rather like a small, neat apartment, even to a well-stocked kitchen. This did not mollify anybody in the party in the slightest. They had not been there more than an hour when a guard let Mea in. The girl seemed subdued.

"I have been sent to ask if you require anything," she said.

"We require a great deal. I want to see Anan Seven."

"He is busy coordinating the casualty lists."

"If he won't talk to me," Kirk said, "he'll have more casualty lists than he knows what to do with."

"Captain, you have your duty to your ship," the girl said quietly. "We have our duty to our planet."

"Your duty doesn't include stepping into a disintegrator and disappearing!"

"I'm afraid it does, Captain," she said, just as quietly as before. "I too have been declared a casualty. I must report to a disintegrator at noon tomorrow."

Kirk stared at her. He still found the whole arrangement impossible to believe. "And you're going to do it? What could Anan and Sar and the others possibly do if you all just refused to show up?"

"It's not a quesion of what the Council would do," Mea said. "If everybody refused to report, Vendikar would have no choice but to launch real weapons—and we would have to do the same. Within a week, there would be nothing left of either civilization. Both planets would be uninhabitable. Surely you can see that ours is the better way."

"No," Kirk said. "I don't see it at all."

"I'm sorry. Is there anything I can bring you?"

"Yes. Anan Seven."

"I'll convey the message. But I doubt that he'll come."

As she left, Kirk pounded a fist into a palm in frustration. Then, suddenly, he had an idea. "Mr. Spock!"

"Yes, sir?"

"Vulcans have limited telepathic abilities, don't they?"

"Yes, Captain," Spock said. "But remember that I am only half Vulcan. I could not reach Anan from here—and if I could, I would not be able to transmit a complex message, or pick one up."

"That isn't what I had in mind. I just want to plant a suspicion in that guard outside. Preferably, that we've cut a hole through the wall with some heat device they overlooked. Or if that's too complex, just a feeling that we're vetting away."

"Hmm," Spock said. "I know nothing about the sensitiveness of the Eminians. However, nothing would be lost by trying."

"Good. Go ahead."

Spock nodded, leaned his head against the wall nearest

the corridor, and closed his eyes. His brow furrowed, and within a few moments he was sweating. Even to Kirk, to whom telepathy was a closed book, it was clear that his first officer was working hard.

Nothing seemed to happen for at least five centuries, or maybe six. Then there was a faint humming at the door, followed by a click. Kirk flattened his back against the wall.

The door swung open and the guard charged in, weapon at the ready. Kirk rewarded him with a crushing blow at the back of the neck; he dropped in complete silence. Kirk dragged him away from the door, retrieving his weapon.

"Thank you, Mr. Spock."

"A pleasure, Captain."

"Now, we've got to get our communicators back, and get in touch with the ship. I don't know how far we'll get without weapons; we'll need more. Mr. Spock, I know how you feel about taking life. But our ship is in danger. Do I make myself clear?"

"Perfectly, Captain. I shall do what is necessary."

Kirk clapped him quickly on the back. "Let's go."

They were perhaps halfway back to the Council chambers when they turned a corner and found themselves on the end of a queue. Kirk signaled a halt and peered ahead.

At the other end of the line was a large enclosed booth, with a control console on one side at which an armed guard was sitting, watching a light over the machine. Presently this went off, and in response to the touch of a control, a door opened in the side of the machine.

The man at the head of the line took a last look around and stepped inside. The door closed. The machine hummed; the light went on, and then off again. The door slid back.

There was nobody inside.

Kirk and Spock exchanged grim looks. Kirk made a pinching motion with one hand, and Spock nodded. Kirk walked rapidly down the side of the queue opposite the side the console and the guard were on.

"All right, break it up," he said. "Stand back, everybody."

Heads turned. The guard half rose. "Just what do you think you're up to . . ." Then he saw Kirk's stolen weapon.

He had courage. Kirk could have shot him easily and he must have known it, but he went for his own gun anyhow. At the same instant Spock, who had scuttled unnoticed down the other side of the line, caught him from behind with his nerve-pinch to the shoulder. Looking astonished, the guard collapsed. Spock scooped up his weapon.

"Excellent, Mr. Spock. The rest of you people, stand back or you'll get hurt."

Kirk leveled his gun at the disintegration booth and pulled the trigger. The results were most satisfying. Nothing seemed to come out of the weapon but a scream of sound, but a huge hole appeared magically in the machine. Sparks flew from the console, and in a moment the booth was in flames.

"All right, now get out of here!" Kirk roared. "Go to your homes and stay there! Go!"

Terrified, the remaining people in the queue turned and ran. Spock joined the Captain, eyeing the gun he had just confiscated with open curiosity, his eyebrows up. "A fascinating weapon. Is it solely sonic, I wonder? If so, how do they keep it in a tight beam?"

"We'll work that out later. Let's get out of here."

There was nobody in the Council room but Anan when they burst in. He was pouring something into a glass from a small bottle. He froze when he saw them, then smoothly resumed the motion and drank.

"Would you care to join me, Captain? You may find our Trova most interesting."

"I didn't come to drink."

Anan nodded toward the weapon in Kirk's hand. "I assume that is what you used to destroy disintegration chamber number twelve."

"Yes. A most efficient weapon—and I'm not at all chary of using it."

"That much is obvious," Anan said. "Clearly you are a barbarian."

"*I* am?" Kirk said incredulously.

20

"Quite. Why not? We all are. Surely in your history too, you were a killer first, a builder second. That is our joint heritage."

"We are a little less cold-blooded about it than you are."

"What does that matter to the dead?" Anan said.

"You have a point. Nevertheless, I don't think you realize the risk you're taking. We don't make war with computers and herd the casualties off to suicide stations. We make the real thing. I could destroy this planet of yours, Councilman. Mr. Spock, Yeoman Manning, see if you can find one of our communicators in this place."

"I already have," Spock said. He handed it over. Anan watched warily.

"Captain," he said, "surely you see the position we are in. If your people do not report to the disintegration chambers, it is a violation of an agreement dating back five hundred years."

"My people are not responsible for your agreements."

"You are an officer of a force charged with keeping the peace," Anan said. He seemed almost to be pleading. "Yet you will be responsible for an escalation that could destroy two worlds. Millions of people horribly killed, complete destruction of our culture and Vendikar's. Disaster, disease, starvation, pain, suffering, lingering death . . ."

"They seem to frighten you," Kirk said grimly.

"They frighten any sane man!"

"Quite so."

"Don't you see?" Anan said desperately. "We've done away with all that! Now you threaten to bring it all down on us again. Do those four hundred people of yours mean more than the hundreds of millions of innocent people on Eminiar and Vendikar? What kind of a monster are you?"

"I'm a barbarian," Kirk said. Nevertheless, this was indeed a nasty impasse. After a moment, he activated the communicator.

"Mr. Scott? Kirk here."

"Captain! We thought they'd got you."

"They thought so too," Kirk said. "What's the situation up there?"

"It's been lively," Scott's voice said. "First they tried to lure us all down with a fake message from you. Luckily, our computer told us the voice-patterns didn't match, though it was a bonny imitation—you'd have enjoyed it. Then they sent us their ultimatum. I dinna have any such orders and I paid no attention."

"Good for you. Then what?"

"When the deadline was past, they opened fire on the *Enterprise*. Of course, after the ultimatum we had our screens up. I wanted to bounce a couple of dozen photon torpedoes off them for a starter—after all, the time was past when they said they were going to kill all of you—but Ambassador Fox wouldna let me. Then he wanted me to let down the screens so he could beam down to the planet and try to patch things up, and *I* wouldna do *that*. Now the haggis is really in the fire as far as he's concerned."

"Scotty, your decisions were entirely proper, and I'll back them to the hilt. I'm going to try to straighten this mess out down here. There's a good chance that I won't succeed. If you don't hear anything to the contrary from me in forty-eight hours, execute General Order Twenty-Four."

"Twenty-Four? But, Captain . . ." There was a long pause. Then Scott's voice said: "In forty-eight hours. Aye, sir. Good luck."

"Thanks. Kirk out."

"And just what," Anan asked, "does that mean?"

"It means that in forty-eight hours, the *Enterprise* will destroy Eminiar Seven."

"You're bluffing. You wouldn't."

"I didn't start this, Councilman," Kirk said. "But I mean to finish it. Now . . ."

He moved to the table and pushed the button he had seen Anan use earlier. The wall slid aside as before, revealing the war room.

"Mr. Spock, see if you can figure that installation out. Anan, you still have something to learn. Destruction. Disease. Suffering. Horror. That's what war is supposed to be, Anan. *That's what makes it a thing to be avoided.* But you've made war neat and painless—so neat and painless that you had no reason to put a stop to it. That's why you've been carrying it on for five hundred years. Any luck, Mr. Spock?"

"Yes, sir," the first officer said. "I cannot read the big

map, but the rest of it seems to be quite straightforward. This unit controls the disintegrator booths; these the attacking devices; this the defense. And these compute the casualties. They are all tied in with a subspace transmission unit, apparently so they are in constant contact with their Vendikan counterparts."

"Is that essential?"

"I would think so, Captain. The minute contact is broken, it would be tantamount to an abrogation of the entire agreement between the two warring parties."

"What are you talking about?" Anan said, in dawning horror.

"This is the key, Captain," Spock said, pointing to an isolated computer. He threw a switch on it, and then another. "The circuit is locked. Destroy this one, and they will all go."

"Good. Stand back. You too, Anan." He raised the stolen disruptor.

"No!" Anan screamed. "No, please . . ."

Kirk fired. The key computer burst. A string of minor explosions seemed to run from it along the main computer bank—and then they were no longer minor. Hastily, Kirk herded everyone out into the corridor. They huddled against the wall, while the floor shook, and billows of smoke surged out of the door of the Council room.

It took a long time. At last, Kirk said, "Well—that's it."

"Do you realize what you've done?" Anan screamed.

"Perfectly. I've given you back the horrors of war. The Vendikans will now assume that you have abandoned your agreement, and will prepare for a real war, with real weapons. The next attack they launch will do a lot more than count up numbers on a computer. It will destroy your cities, devastate your planet. You'll want to retaliate, of course. If I were you I'd start making bombs."

"You *are* a monster," Anan whispered.

Kirk ignored him. "Yes, Councilman, you've got a real war on your hands. You can either wage it—with real weapons—or you might consider the alternative."

"There is no alternative."

"There is," Kirk said harshly. "Make peace."

"After five hundred years of casualties? You're mad!"

"Maybe. But we too have killed in the past, as you pointed out a while ago. Nevertheless, we can stop. We can admit we have been killers—but we're not going to kill today. That's all it takes; one simple decision. We are not going to kill today."

Anan put a shaking hand to his forehead. "I don't know . . . I can't see . . ."

"We'll help you." He raised the communicator. "Scotty, have you and Ambassador Fox been following this conversation? I left the line open for you."

"Aye, that we have."

"Then you can beam the Ambassador down here if you want."

After a moment, there was a shimmer in the chamber, and Fox materialized, looking portly and confused.

"This is what you do," Kirk told Anan. "Contact Vendikar. I think you'll find that they're just as terrified and appalled as you are at the prospects. They'll do anything to avoid the alternative I've just given you; peace—or utter destruction. It's up to you."

Anan looked at them all, hope fighting with despair on his face. Ambassador Fox stepped forward.

"Councilman," he said, "as a third party, interested only in peace and the establishment of normal relations, I will be glad to offer my services as a negotiator between you and Vendikar. I have had some small experience in these matters."

Anan took a step toward him. "Perhaps," he muttered. "Perhaps there may be time. I have a direct channel to the Vendikar High Council. It hasn't been used in centuries."

"Then it's long overdue," the Ambassador said. "If you'll be so kind as to lead the way . . ."

Anan started hesitantly down the corridor, his steps beginning to regain their springiness. Fox followed closely. Anan said, "I understand the head of the Vendikar Council—his name is Ripoma—is an intelligent man. And if he hears from a disinterested party like yourself . . ."

His voice became unintelligible as they rounded a corner. The rest of the *Enterprise* party watched them go.

"There is a chance it will work, Captain," Spock said. "Much depends upon the approach and the conduct of the negotiations, of course."

"Annoying though he is, Ambassador Fox has a reputation for being good at his job," Kirk said. "I'm glad he's going to be good for something at last." He raised the communicator once more. "Kirk to *Enterprise*. Cancel General Order Twenty-Four. Alert transporter room. Ready to beam up in ten minutes."

"Aye, sir."

"Still, Captain," Spock said, "you took a very big chance."

"Did I, Mr. Spock? They were killing three million people a year—and it had gone on for five hundred years. An actual attack might not have killed any more people than the fifteen hundred million they've already killed in their computer attacks—but it would have destroyed their ability to make war. The fighting would be over. Permanently."

"I would not care to have counted on that," Spock said.

"I wasn't, Mr. Spock. It was only a calculated risk. What I was really counting upon was that the Eminians keep a very orderly society—and actual war is very messy. Very, very messy. I had a feeling they'd do anything to avoid it—even talk peace!"

"A feeling, Captain? Intuition?"

"No," Kirk said. "Call it . . . shall we say, cultural morphology?"

If Spock had any answer, it was lost in the shimmer of the transporter effect.

TOMORROW IS YESTERDAY
(D. C. Fontana)

The star was very old—as old as it is possible for a star to be, a first-generation star, born when the present universe was born. It had had all the experiences possible for a star—it had had planets; had gone nova, wiping out those planets and all those who lived upon them; had become an X-ray star; then a neutron star. At last, slowly collapsing upon itself into an ultimately dense mass of pseudomatter resembling—except for its compaction—the primordial ylem out of which it had been created—it drew its gravitational field in so closely about itself that not even the few dim red flickers of light left to it could get out, and it prepared to die.

The star was still there, still in its orbit, and still incredibly massive despite its shrunken volume; but it could no longer be seen or detected. It would soon be in a space all its own, a tiny sterile universe as uninteresting and forgotten as a burial jug. It had become a black star.

The *Enterprise,* on a rare trip back toward the Sol sector and Earth, hit the black star traveling at warp factor four—sixty-four times the speed of light.

It could not, of course, properly be said that the *Enterprise* hit the black star itself. Technically, the bubble of subspace in which the *Enterprise* was enclosed, which would have been moving at 64C had the bubble impossibly been in normal space at all, hit that part of the black star's gravitational cocoon that had also begun to extrude into subspace. The technicalities, however, are not very convincing. Since no such thing had ever happened to a starship before, nobody could have predicted it, and the theoreticians are still arguing about just *why* the collision produced the results it did.

About the results themselves, nobody is in any doubt.

Captain Kirk dragged himself up from unconsciousness and shook his head to clear it. This was a mistake, and he did not try it a second time. The bridge was dim and quiet; the main lights were off, so was the screen, and only a few telltales glowed on the boards. Crew personnel —Spock, Uhura, Sulu—were slumped in their seats; Ames, the security chief, was spilled crookedly on the deck. It looked like the aftermath of a major attack.

"Spock!"

The first officer stirred, and then got shakily to his feet. "Here, Captain. What in the nine worlds . . ."

"I don't know. Everything was normal, and then, blooey! Check us out."

"Right." In immediate control of himself, Spock ran a quick check of his library computer. Except for a few flickers here and there on the board, it was dead, as Kirk could see himself. Spock abandoned it without a second thought and went promptly to Uhura.

"Except for secondary systems, everything is out, sir," he said. "We are on impulse power only. If Mr. Scott is still with us, the auxiliaries should be on in a moment. Are you all right, Lieutenant?"

Uhura nodded wordlessly and smiled at him, though it was not a very convincing smile. At the same moment, the main lights flickered on, brightened and steadied. A hum of computers and pumps began to fill in the familiar, essential background noise that was as much a part of life on the *Enterprise* as the air.

"Mr. Scott," Spock said, straightening, "is still with us."

Sulu sat up groggily, also shook his head, and also apparently decided against trying the experiment a second time. Kirk flicked a switch on his chair panel.

"This is the captain," he said. "Damage control parties on all decks, check in. All departments tie in to the library computer. Report casualties and operational readiness to the first officer. Kirk out. Miss Uhura, contact Starfleet control. Whatever we hit in the Base Nine area, I want them alerted—and maybe they'll know something about it we don't. Mr. Spock?"

Spock half-turned from his station, an earphone still to one ear. "Only minor injuries to the crew, Captain. All decks operating on auxiliary systems. Engineering reports warp engines nonoperational. Mr. Scott overrode the automatic helm setting and is using impulse power to hold us in fixed orbit, but . . ."

"Fixed orbit around what, Mr. Spock?"

"The Earth, sir. I am at present unable to say how we got here."

"Screen on," Kirk said.

The screen came on. It was the Earth below them, all right.

"We're too low in the atmosphere to retain this altitude," Spock said. "Engineer reports we have enough impulse power to achieve escape velocity."

"Helm, give us some altitude."

"Yes, sir," Sulu said. "Helm answers. She's sluggish, sir."

"Sir," Uhura said. "Normal Starfleet channel has nothing on it but static. I'm picking up something on another frequency, but it's not identifiable."

"Put it on audio, Lieutenant."

Uhura flicked a tumbler and the loudspeaker on her board burst out: ". . . five-thirty news summary. Cape Kennedy—the first manned moon shot is scheduled for Wednesday, six A.M., Eastern Standard Time. All three astronauts set to make this historic flight are . . ."

Kirk was up out of his chair on the instant. "The first manned moon shot!" he said. "You've got some sort of dramatization. That shot was back in the 1970s."

Uhura nodded and tried another channel, but from the computer, Spock said slowly: "Apparently, Captain, so are we."

"Mr. Spock, this is no time for joking."

"I never joke," Spock said severely. "At present I have only rough computations, but apparently what we hit was the subspace component of an intense spherical gravity field, very likely a black star. The field translated our momentum in terms of time—a relativistic effect. I can give you an exact reading in a few moments, but 1970 seems to be of about the right order of magnitude."

Kirk sat down again, stunned. Uhura continued scanning. Finally she said, "Captain, I'm picking up a ground-to-air transmission in this sector."

"Verified," Spock said. "Our scanners are picking up some kind of craft approaching from below us, under cloud cover and closing fast."

The loudspeaker said: "Blue Jay Four, this is Black Jack. We're tracking both you and the UFO."

28

"I have him on my screen," another voice said. "Following."

"Good, let's get this one for once."

"Mr. Sulu," Kirk said, "can we gain altitude faster?"

"I'm trying, sir, but she's still slow in responding."

"Blue Jay Four, have you got visual contact yet?"

"I can see it fine," said the second voice. "And it's huge too. As big as a cruiser, bigger maybe. It *is* saucer-shaped, but there're two cylindrical projections on top and one below."

"We have two more flights scrambled and on the way," said the first voice. "They'll rendezvous with you in two minutes."

"Won't be here, Black Jack. The UFO is climbing away fast."

"Blue Jay Four, close on the object and force it to land. We want it down—or at least disabled until the other planes arrive. After thirty years of rumors, this may be our first clear shot."

"Acknowledged. Closing in."

"Can he harm us?" Kirk said.

"I would judge so, Captain," Spock said. "The aircraft is an interceptor equipped with missiles, possibly armed with nuclear warheads. Since we do not have the power for a full screen, he could at least damage us severely."

"Scotty!" Kirk said into his microphone. "Activate tractor beam. Lock onto that aircraft and hold it out there."

"Captain," Spock said, "that type of aircraft may be too fragile to take tractor handling."

"Tractor on, sir," Scott's voice said briskly. "We have the target."

Spock looked into his hooded viewer and shook his head. "And it is breaking up, Captain."

"Transporter room! Can you lock on the cockpit of that aircraft?"

"No problem, Captain."

"Beam that pilot aboard," Kirk said, springing up. "Spock, take over."

The figure who materialized in the transporter chamber was a strange sight to Kirk until he removed his oxygen mask and helmet. Then he was revealed as a medium-tall,

29

compactly built man with an expression of grim determination despite his obvious amazement. He would have made a good starship crewman, Kirk thought . . . centuries from now.

"Welcome to the *Enterprise*," Kirk said, smiling.

"You . . . you speak English!"

"That's right," Kirk said. "You can step down from our transporters, Mr. . . . ?"

"Captain John Christopher," the pilot said stiffly. "United States Air Force, serial number 4857932. And that's all the information you get."

"Relax, Captain. You're among friends. I'm Captain James T. Kirk, and I apologize for bringing you aboard so abruptly. But we had no choice. I didn't know your ship couldn't hold up under our tractor beam until it was too late."

"Don't give me any double-talk," Christopher said. "I demand to know . . ."

"You're in no position to demand anything, but we'll answer all your questions anyhow in good time. Meanwhile, relax. You're our guest. I have a feeling you'll find it interesting."

He led the way out of the transporter room. Christopher shrugged and followed. As they moved down the corridor, he was obviously missing nothing; clearly a trained observer. When a pretty young crew-woman carrying a tricorder went past them, however, he had trouble retaining his composure. "Passenger?" he said.

"No, crew. About a fourth of the crew is female—exactly a hundred at the moment."

"A crew of four hundred?"

"Four hundred and thirty. Now if you'll step aboard the elevator . . ."

Christopher did, and was immediately startled once more when it moved horizontally instead of up or down. After digesting this peculiarity, he said:

"It must have taken quite a lot of money to build a ship like this."

"Indeed it did. There are only twelve like it in the fleet."

"The fleet? Did the Navy . . . ?"

"We're a combined service, Captain," Kirk said. "Our authority is the United Federation of Planets."

"Federation of—Planets?"

"That's right. Actually, Captain—this is a little difficult to explain. We . . . we're from your future. A time warp landed us back here. It was an accident."

"You people seem to have a lot of them," Christopher said drily, "if all the UFO reports stem from the same kind of source. However, I can't argue with the fact that you *are* here, ship and all." While he spoke, the elevator doors snapped open to reveal the bridge, with Spock in the command chair. "And I've never believed in little green men."

"Neither have I," Spock said, rising.

This time Christopher made no attempt to conceal his astonishment. *And Spock claims he never jokes,* Kirk thought; but he said only, "Captain Christopher, this is my first officer, Commander Spock."

"Captain," Spock said with an abrupt but courteous nod.

"Please feel free to look around the bridge, Captain. I'm sure you have the good sense not to touch anything. I think you'll find it interesting."

" 'Interesting,' " Christopher said, "is not a very adequate word for it." He moved over toward the communications and library-computer stations, but could not help shooting another look at Spock as he did so. Kirk did not explain; everybody else on board took the half-alien first officer as a matter of course, and Christopher might as well practice doing the same; he might be with them for quite a while yet.

"We have achieved a stable orbit out of Earth's atmosphere, Captain," Spock said. "Our deflector shields are operative now, and ought to prevent us from being picked up again as a UFO." He made a grimace of distaste over the word. "Mr. Scott wishes to speak to you about the engines."

"Very well, Mr. Spock. I know that expression. What else is on your mind?"

"Captain Christopher."

Kirk looked toward the newcomer. He was talking to Uhura; the spectacle of a beautiful Bantu girl operating a communications board evidently had diverted him, at least temporarily, from the first officer.

"All right, what about him?"

"We cannot return him to Earth," Spock said. "He already knows too much about us and is learning more. I mean no aspersions on his character, about which I know nothing, but suppose an unscrupulous man were to gain possession of the knowledge of man's certain future, as represented by us? Such a man could speculate—manipulate key industries, stocks, even nations—and in doing so, change what must be. And if it is changed, Captain, you and I and everything we know might be made impossible."

"We'd just vanish? Including thousands of tons of *Enterprise?*"

"Like a soap bubble."

"Hmm. You know, Spock, your logic can be very annoying." Kirk looked back at Christopher. "That flight suit must be uncomfortable. Have the quartermaster issue Captain Christopher some suitable clothes—tactfully relieving him of any sidearms he may be carrying in the process—and then I want to see you and him in my quarters."

"Yes, sir."

Kirk was talking to the computer when they came in; he waved them to seats. "Captain's log, supplemental. Engineering Officer Scott reports warp engines damaged but repairable. Ascertain precise degree and nature of damage, compute nature and magnitude of forces responsible, and program possible countermeasures."

"Affirm; operating," said the computer's voice in midair. Christopher did not react; evidently he was getting used to surprises.

"Kirk out. Now, Captain, we have a problem. To put the matter bluntly, what are we going to do with you? We can't put you back."

"What do you mean, can't? Mr. Spock here tells me that your transporter can work over even longer distances than this."

"It's not the transporter," Kirk said. "You know what the future looks like, Captain. If anybody else finds out, they could change the course of it—and destroy it."

"I can see that," Christopher said after a moment. "But it also strikes me that my disappearance would also change things."

"Apparently not," Spock said. "I have run a computer check through all historical tapes. They show no relevant contribution by any Captain John Christopher. There was a popular author by that name, but it was a pen name; you are not he."

Christopher was visibly deflated, but not for long. He stood and began to pace. Finally he swung back toward Kirk.

"Captain," he said, "if it were only a matter of my own preference, I'd stay. I'd give my right arm to learn more about this ship—*all* about it. It's a colossal achievement and obviously it implies even greater ones in the background. But my preference doesn't count. It's my duty to report what I've seen. I have an oath to uphold." He paused, then added pointedly: "What would you do?"

"Just that," Kirk said. "I entirely understand. You are the kind of man we recruit for our own service, and can never get enough of, though we don't have oaths any more. But unfortunately, this means that you are also of superior intelligence. We cannot risk any report that you might make."

"I have a wife and two children," Christopher said quietly. "I suppose that makes no difference to you."

"It makes a lot of difference to me," Kirk said. "But I cannot let it sway me."

"In both your trades—the pilot and the warrior—there was always an unusually high risk that you would become a casualty," Spock said. "You knew it when you married; so did your wife. You bet against the future, with high odds against you. Unfortunately, we are the future and you have lost; you are, in effect, now a casualty."

"Mr. Spock is no more unfeeling than I am," Kirk added. "But logic is one of his specialties, and what he says is quite true. I can only say I'm sorry, and I mean it." The intercom interrupted him. "Excuse me a moment. Kirk here."

"Engineer here, Captain. Everything's jury-rigged, but we're coming along with the repairs and should be ready to reenergize in four hours."

"Good. Scotty, you can fix anything."

"Except broken hearts, maybe. But, sir . . ."

"What is it? Plow right ahead."

"Well, sir," Scott's voice said, "I can fix the engines,

but I canna build you a time machine. We'll be ready to go, but we've no place *to* go in this era. Mister Spock tells me that in the 1970s the human race was wholly confined to the Earth. Space outside the local group of stars was wholly dominated by the Vegan Tyranny, and you'll recall what happened when we first hit *them*. D'ye see the problem?"

"I'm afraid," Kirk said heavily, "that I do. Very well, Mr. Scott, carry on."

"Yes, sir. Out."

Christopher's face was a study in bitter triumph; but what he said next, oddly, was obviously designed to be helpful—or at least, to establish that his own hope was well-founded.

"Mr. Spock here tells me that he is half Vulcan. Surely ou can reach Vulcan from here. That's supposed to be just inside the orbit of Mercury."

"There is no such solar planet as Vulcan," Kirk said. Mr. Spock's father was a native of The Vulcan, which is a planet of 40 Eridani. Of course we could reach that too . . ."

". . . but in the 1970's," Spock finished. "If we took the *Enterprise* there, we would unwrite *their* future history too. Captain, this is the most perfect case of General Order Number One that I have ever encountered—or think I am likely to encounter."

"The order," Kirk explained to Christopher, "prohibits interference with the normal development of alien life and alien societies. It hadn't occurred to me until Mr. Spock mentioned it, but I'm sure it would be construed to ιpply here too."

"Too bad, Captain," Christopher said. He was not bothering to conceal his triumph now. "Maybe I can't go ʰome—but neither can you. You're as much a prisoner in t·me as I am on this ship."

"I believe, sir," Spock said, "that Captain Christopher's summary is quite exact."

It was indeed exact, but not complete, as Kirk quickly realized. There was also the problem of supplies. The *Enterprise* could never land on any planet—and certainly would not dare to land on this one, its own home world, even if it were possible—and it was simply ridiculous to even consider trying to steal food, water and power by gig

34

or transporter for 430 people. As for Christopher—who had already tried to escape through the transporter and had come perilously close to making it—what prospects did he have if the *Enterprise* somehow did get back to its own time? He would be archaic, useless, a curiosity. Possibly he could be retrained sufficiently to find a niche, but never retrained to forget his wife and children. To check that, Kirk visited McCoy, the ship's surgeon.

"Get him down here and I'll check," McCoy said.

Kirk put in the call. "You mean it *might* be done?"

"It depends upon the depth of his commitment. Some marriages are routine. I'll have to see what the electroencephalograph shows."

"You're starting to sound like Spock."

"If you're going to get nasty, I'll leave."

Kirk grinned, but the grin faded quickly. "If the depth of his commitment is crucial, we're sunk. He's the kind who commits himself totally. Witness yesterday's escape attempt."

Spock came in with the prisoner—after the escape attempt, there was no other honest word for it. He said at once:

"Captain, I do not know what Dr. McCoy has in mind, but I think it may be useless by now; I have some new information. I find I made an error in my computations."

"This," McCoy said drily, "could be a historic occasion."

Spock ignored the surgeon. "I find that we must return Captain Christopher to Earth after all."

"You said I made no relative contributions." Christopher said sourly.

"I was speaking of cultural contributions. I have now checked the genetic contributions, which was a serious oversight. In running a cross-check on that factor, I discovered that your son, Colonel Shaun Geoffrey Christopher, headed . . . *will* head the first successful Earth-Titan probe, which is certainly significant. If Captain Christopher is not returned, there won't be any Colonel Christopher to go to the Saturnian satellites, since the boy does not yet exist."

The grin on Christopher's face made him look remarkably like a Halloween pumpkin. "A boy," he said, to nobody in particular. "I'm going to have a son."

"And we," McCoy said, "have a headache."

"No," Kirk said. "We have an obligation. Two obligations, mutually antagonistic."

"It is possible that we can satisfy both of them at once," Spock said.

"How? Out with it, man!"

"I have the data you ordered the computer to work out, and there is now no question but that the only reason we are here at all is because we had a head-on collision with a black star. To get back home, we are going to have to contrive something similar."

"Do you know of any black stars around here? And how will that solve our problem with Captain Christopher?"

"There is a black star quite nearby, in fact, Captain, but we cannot use it because it is well out of transporter range of Earth. That would prevent our returning Captain Christopher. But Engineering Officer Scott thinks we may be able to use our own sun. It will, he says, be a rough ride, but will also offer us certain advantages. Briefly, if we make a close hyperbolic passage around the sun at warp eight . . ."

"Not with *my* ship," Kirk said coldly.

"Please, Captain, hear me out. We need the velocity because we must compensate for the Sun's relatively weak gravitational field. And I spoke of advantages. What will happen, if nothing goes wrong, is that we will retreat further into time as we reach the head of the hyperbola . . ."

"Just what we need," McCoy said.

"Shut up, Bones, I want to hear this."

". . . and as we mount the other leg of the curve, there will be a slingshot effect that will hurl us forward in time again. If this is most precisely calculated, we will pass within transporter range of the Earth within two or three minutes *before* the time when we arrived here the first time, before we first appeared in the sky. At that moment, we reinject Captain Christopher into his plane—which will not have been destroyed yet—and the whole chain of consequences will fall apart. Essentially, it will never have happened at all."

"Are you sure of that?"

Spock raised his eyebrows. "No, sir, of course I am not sure of it. Mr. Scott and I think it may work. The computer concurs. Certainty is not an attainable goal in a problem like this."

"True enough," Kirk agreed. "But I don't see that it solves our problem with Captain Christopher at all. It gets him back home, but with his memories intact—and that's what we have to avoid at all costs. I would rather destroy the *Enterprise* than the future."

There was a brief silence. Both Spock and McCoy knew well what such a decision had cost him. Then Spock said gently, "Captain, Mr. Scott and I see no such necessity. Bear in mind that Captain Christopher will arrive home *before* he was taken aboard our ship. He will have nothing to remember—because none of it will ever have happened."

Kirk turned to the pilot from the past. "Does that satisfy you?"

"Do I have a choice?" Christopher said. "Well, I won't quibble. It gets me home—and obviously I can't do my duty if I can't remember what it is. Only . . ."

"Only what?"

"Well, I never thought I'd make it into space. I was in line for the space program, but I didn't qualify."

"Take a good look around, Captain," Kirk said quietly. "You made it here ahead of all of them. We were not the first. You were."

"Yes, I know that," Christopher said, staring down at his clenched fists. "And I've seen the future too. An immense gift. I . . . I'll be very sorry to forget it."

"How old are you?" McCoy said abruptly.

"Eh? I'm thirty."

"Then, Captain Christopher," McCoy said, "in perhaps sixty more years, or a few more, you will forget things many times more important to you than this—your wife, your children, and indeed the very fact that you ever existed at all. You will forget every single thing you ever loved, and what is worse, you will not even care."

"Is that," Christopher said angrily, "supposed to be consoling? If that's a sample of the philosophy of the future, I can do without it."

"I am not counseling despair," McCoy said, very gently. "I am only trying to remind you that regardless of our achievements, we all at last go down into the dark. I am a doctor and I have seen a great deal of death. It

37

doesn't discourage me. On the contrary, I'm trying to call to your attention the things that are much more valuable to you than the fact that you've seen men from the future and a bucketful of gadgetry. You will have those still, though you forget us. We are trying to give them back to you, those sixty-plus years you might otherwise have wasted in a future you could never understand. The fact that you will have to forget this encounter in the process seems to me to be a very small fee."

Christopher stared at McCoy as though he had never seen him before. After a long pause, he said, "I was wrong. Even if I did remember, I would do nothing to destroy a future that . . . that has even one such man in it. And I see that underneath all your efficiency and gadgetry, you're *all* like that. I am proud to be one of your ancestors. Captain Kirk, I concur in anything you decide."

"Your bravery helped to make us whatever we are," Kirk said. "Posts, everybody."

"And besides," Spock added, "it is quite possible that we won't make it at all."

"Now there," McCoy said, "is a philosophy *I* can do without."

Kirk said evenly, "We will take the chance that we have. If you'll join me on the bridge, Captain Christopher, we will at least give you a bumpy last ride for your money."

Christopher grinned. "That's the kind I like."

It was indeed a bumpy ride. Warp Eight was an acceleration called upon only in the most extreme of emergencies—although this surely classified as one—and could not be sustained for long without serious damage to the *Enterprise*. It was decidedly unsettling to hear the whole monstrous fabric of the ship, which ordinarily seemed as solid as a planet, creaking and straining around them as the pressure was applied, and to hear the engines—usually quite quiet—howling below decks.

For Kirk, it was almost more unsettling to watch the planets begin to both revolve and rotate in the wrong direction in the navigation tank, as the combined acceleration and gravitational energies were translated into motion backwards in time. Perhaps fortunately for his sanity, he did not have to watch long, however, for the close approach to the sun eventually made it necessary to close off all outside sensors. They were flying blind.

Then the swing was completed, and the sensors could be opened again—and now the planets were moving in their proper directions, but rather decidedly too fast, as the *Enterprise* shot up the time curve. In the Transporter Room, Captain Christopher waited tensely, in full flight dress.

"Passing 1968," Spock said from his post. "January 1969 . . . March . . . May . . . July . . . the pace is picking up very rapidly . . . November . . ."

Kirk gripped the arms of his chair. This was going to have to be the most split-second of all Transporter shots. No human operator could hope to bring it off; the actual shift would be under the control of the computer.

"June . . . August . . . December . . . into 1970 now—"

Suddenly, and only for an instant, the lights dimmed. It was over so quickly that it could almost have been an illusion.

"Transporter Room! Did you—?"

But there was no time to complete the question. The lights dimmed again, all the stars in the heavens seemed to be scrambling for new places, and there was a huge wrench in what seemed to be the whole fabric of the universe.

At last the stars were stable—and the instruments showed the *Enterprise* to be doing no more than Warp One. The gigantic thrust had all been drained off into time.

"Well, Mr. Spock?"

"We made it, sir," Spock said quietly.

"Transporter Room, did you get a picture of the shot?"

"Yes, sir. Here it is."

The still picture glowed on an auxiliary screen. Kirk studied it. It showed Captain Christopher in the cockpit of his undestroyed airplane. He looked quite unharmed, though perhaps a bit dazed.

"And so we have revised Omar," Mr. Spock said.

"Omar?" Kirk said. "Which part?"

"The verse about the moving finger, sir. The poet says that once it writes, it moves on, and we have no power to unwrite a line of it. But it would appear, sir, that we have."

"No," Kirk said, "I don't think that's the case. History has *not* been changed—and it's quite possible that we would have been unable to do anything else than what we in fact did. That's a question for the philosophers. But as of now, Mr. Spock, I think Omar's laurels are still in place."

ERRAND OF MERCY
(Gene L. Coon)

The Klingon scout ship must have known that it was no match whatsoever for the *Enterprise*—after all, the Klingons were experts in such matters. But it fired on the *Enterprise* anyhow as Kirk's ship approached Organia.

The Federation ship's phasers promptly blew the scout into very small flinders, but the attack was a measure of the Klingons' determination to bar the Federation from using Organia as a base. Organia was of no intrinsic value to either side—largely farmland, worked by a people with neither any skill at, nor interest in, fighting—but strategically it was the only Class M planet in the disputed zone, over which negotiations had already broken down. It was, Kirk thought, another Armenia, another Belgium—the weak innocents who always turn out to be located on a natural invasion route.

And the scout ship had had plenty of time to get off a message before opening fire. It had to be assumed that a Klingon fleet was now on the way, if there hadn't been one on the way already. That left very little time for negotiating with the Organians.

Leaving Sulu in charge of the *Enterprise*—with strict orders to cut and run if any Klingon fleet showed up—Kirk and Spock beamed down. The street in which they arrived might have been that of any English village of the thirteenth century: thatched roofs, a few people wearing rude homespun, a brace of oxen pulling a crude wagon. In the distance, something that looked like a ruined castle or fortress, old and decayed, but massive, glowered over the village—an odd construction for a culture that was supposed to have no history of warfare. As for the passersby, they paid no attention to the two starship officers, as if they were used to seeing men beaming down every day. That too seemed rather unlikely.

When the reception committee finally arrived, however, it was cordial enough. It consisted of three smiling, elderly men in fur-trimmed robes, who introduced themselves as Ayelborne, Trefayne and Claymare. Kirk and Spock were received in a small room with roughly plastered walls and no decorations, and containing only a rude table flanked by plain chairs.

Spock lowered his tricorder. "Absolutely no energy output anywhere," he murmured to the Captain. Kirk nodded; the report only confirmed his own impression. This was not a medieval culture making progress toward mechanization, as the original reports had indicated. It was totally stagnant—a laboratory specimen of an arrested culture. Most peculiar.

"My government," he told the smiling Organians, "has informed me that the Klingons are expected to move against your planet, with the objective of making it a base of operations against our Federation. My mission, frankly, is to try to keep them from doing this."

"What you are saying," Ayelborne said, "is that we seem to have a choice between dealing with you or your enemies." In another context the words might have seemed hostile, but Ayelborne was still smiling.

"No, sir. With the Federation you will have a choice. You will have none with the Klingons. They are a military dictatorship, to which war is a way of life. We offer you protection."

"Thank you," Ayelborne said. "But we do not need your protection. We have nothing anyone could want."

"You have this planet, and its strategic location. If you don't move to prevent it, the Klingons will move in, just as surely as your sun sets. We'll help you with your defenses, build facilities . . ."

"We have no defenses, Captain, nor are any needed," the man called Claymare said.

"Excuse me, but you're wrong. I've seen what the Klingons do to planets like yours. They are organized into vast slave labor camps. You'll have no freedom whatsoever. Your goods will be confiscated. Hostages will be taken and killed. Your leaders will be confined. You'd be better off on a penal planet."

"Captain," Ayelborne said, "we see that your concern is genuine, and we appreciate it. But again we assure you that there is absolutely no danger . . ."

"I assure you that there is! Do you think I'm lying? Why?"

"You did not let me finish," Ayelborne said gently. "I was going to say, there is no danger to ourselves. You and your friend are in danger, certainly. It would be best for you to return to your ship as soon as possible."

"Gentlemen, I beg you to reconsider. We can be of immense help to you. In addition to the military assistance, we can send in technicians, specialists. We can show you how to feed a thousand people where you fed one before. We'll build schools and help you educate your young, teach them what we know—your public facilities seem to be almost nonexistent. We could remake your world, end disease, hunger, hardship. But we are forbidden to help you if you refuse to be helped."

"A moving plea," Trefayne said. "But . . ."

He was interrupted by the beeping of Kirk's communicator. "Excuse me, sir," he said. "Kirk here."

"Captain," said Sulu's voice. "A large number of Klingon vessels just popped out of subspace around us. I didn't get a count before they opened fire but there must be at least twenty. My screens are up now, and I can't drop them to beam you aboard."

"You're not supposed to," Kirk said harshly. "Your orders are to run for it and contact the fleet. Come back only if you've got better odds. Mark and move!"

He switched off and stared at the three Organians.

"You kept insisting that there was no danger. Now . . ."

"We are already aware of the Klingon fleet," Trefayne said. "There are in fact eight more such vessels now assuming orbit around our planet."

"Can you verify that, Spock?"

"No, sir, not at this distance," Spock said. "But it seems a logical development."

"Ah," Trefayne added. "Several hundred armed men have just appeared near the citadel."

Spock aimed his tricorder in that direction and nodded. "Not just hand weapons, either," he said. "I am picking up three or four pieces of heavy-duty equipment. How did he know that so quickly, I wonder?"

"That doesn't matter now," Kirk said grimly. "What matters is that we're stranded here, right in the middle of the Klingon occupation army."

"So it would seem, sir," Spock said. "Not a pleasant prospect."

"Mr. Spock," Kirk said, "you have a gift for understatement."

The Klingons were hard-faced, hard-muscled men, originally of Oriental stock. They were indeed heavily armed and wore what looked like vests of mail. They moved purposefully and efficiently through the streets, posting guards as they went. The few Organians they met smiled at them and moved quietly, passively out of their way.

To compound Kirk's bafflement, the uncooperative Organian council—if that is what the three men were—had provided him and Spock with Organian clothing and offered to conceal them, an offer entailing colossal risks. Then, rummaging through the discarded uniforms, Kirk demanded suddenly: "Where are our weapons?"

"We took them, Captain," Ayelborne said. "We cannot permit violence here. Claymare, remove the uniforms. No, we will have to protect you ourselves. Mr. Spock presents the chief problem. He will have to pose as a Vulcan trader—perhaps here to deal in kevas and trillium."

"They're aware that Vulcan is a member of the Federation," Kirk said.

"But harmless to the Klingons. You, Captain, might well be an Organian citizen, if . . ."

He got no further. The door flew open, and two Klingon soldiers burst in, gesturing with handguns for everyone to back up. They were followed by a third Klingon, an erect, proud man, who did not need his commander's insignia to show who he was.

Spock and the Organians retreated; Kirk stood his ground. The Klingon commander looked quickly around the room.

"*This* is the ruling council?" he said contemptuously.

Ayelborne stepped forward again, smiling. "I am Ayelborne, temporary council head. I bid you welcome."

"No doubt you do. I am Kor, military governor of Organia." He glared at Kirk. "Who are you?"

"He is Baroner," Ayelborne said. "One of our leading citizens. This is Trefayne . . ."

"This Baroner has no tongue?"

"I have a tongue," Kirk said.

"Good. When I address you, you will answer. Where is your smile?"

"My what?"

"The stupid, idiotic smile everyone else seems to be wearing." Kor swung on Spock. "A Vulcan. Do you also have a tongue?"

"My name is Spock. I am a dealer in kevas and trillium."

"You don't look like a storekeeper. What is trillium?"

Spock said smoothly, and with an impassive face: "A medicinal plant of the lily family."

"Not on Organia, it isn't," Kor said. "Obviously a Federation spy. Take him to the examination room."

"He's no spy," Kirk said angrily.

"Well, well," Kor said. "Have we a ram among the sheep? Why do you object to us taking him? He's not even human."

Kirk caught the warning glance Spock was trying to disguise and made a major effort to control himself as well. "He has done nothing, that's all."

"Coming from an Organian, yours is practically an act of rebellion. Very good. They welcome me. Do you also welcome me?"

"You're here," Kirk said. "I can't do anything about it."

Kor stared hard at him, and then permitted himself a faint smile. "Good honest hatred," he said. "Very refreshing. However, it makes no difference whether you welcome me or not. I am here and I will stay. You are now subjects of the Klingon Empire. You will find there are many rules and regulations, which will be posted. Violation of the smallest of them will be punished by death; we will have no time for justice just now."

"Your regulations will be obeyed," Ayelborne said.

Kirk felt his mouth tightening. Kor saw it; apparently he missed very little. He said:

"You disapprove, Baroner?"

"Do you need my approval?"

"I need your obedience, nothing more," Kor said softly. "Will I have it?"

"You seem to be in command," Kirk said, shrugging.

"How true." Kor began to pace. "Now, I shall need a

representative from among you, liaison between the forces of occupation and the civilian population. I don't trust men who smile too much. Baroner, you are appointed."

"Me?" Kirk said. "I don't want the job."

"Have I asked whether or not you wanted it? As for the rest of you—we Klingons have a reputation for ruthlessness. You will find that it is deserved. Should one Klingon soldier be killed here, a thousand Organians will die. I will have *order,* is that clear?"

"Commander," Ayelborne said, "I assure you we will cause you no trouble."

"No. I am sure you will not. Baroner, come with me."

"What about Mr. Spock?"

"Why are you concerned?"

"He's my friend."

"You have poor taste in friends. He will be examined. If he is lying, he will die. If he is telling the truth, well, he will find that business has taken a turn for the worse. Guards, remove him."

The guards, covering Spock with their weapons, gestured him out the door; Spock went meekly. Kirk started after him, only to be shoved back by Kor himself. Kirk could not help flushing, but Kor only nodded.

"You do not like to be pushed," the Klingon said. "Good. At least you are a man I can understand. Come with me."

Kor had set up shop in the citadel Kirk and Spock had seen on their first arrival. Seen close up, and from inside, the impression it gave of vast age was intensified. Kor had furnished one room with a large Klingon insignia, a desk, one chair, and nothing else; Kirk stood. Kor signed a document and thrust it across the desk at him.

"For duplication and posting," he said. "From this day on, no public assemblages of more than three people. All publications to be cleared through this office. Neighborhood controls will be established. Hostages selected. A somewhat lengthy list of crimes against the state."

Kirk glanced impassively at the list, aware that Kor as usual was watching him closely. The commander said: "You do not like them?"

"Did you expect me to?"

Kor only grinned. At the same time, the door opened

and Spock was thrust inside, followed by a Klingon lieutenant. To Kirk's enormous relief, his first officer looked perfectly normal.

"Well, lieutenant?"

"He is what he claims to be, Commander," the lieutenant said. "A Vulcan trader named Spock. And he really is trading in the other kind of trillium, the vegetable kind; it seems it has value here."

"Nothing else?"

"The usual apprehension. His main concern seems to be how he will carry on his business under our occupation. His mind is so undisciplined that he could hold nothing back."

"All right. Baroner, would you like to try our little truth-finder?"

"I don't even understand it."

"It's a mind-sifter," Kor said, "or a mind-ripper, depending on how much force is used. If necessary, we can empty a man's mind as if opening a spigot. Of course, what's left is more vegetable than human."

"You're proud of it?" Kirk said.

"All war weapons are unpleasant," Kor said. "Otherwise they would be useless."

"Mr. Spock, are you sure you're all right?"

"Perfectly, Baroner. However, it was a remarkable sensation."

"That's enough," Kor said, with a trace of suspicion in his voice. "Vulcan, you can go. But just bear in mind that you're an enemy alien, and will be under scrutiny at all times."

"Quite, Commander," Spock said. "I understand you very well."

"Baroner, return to your council and get that proclamation posted. Until the people know what's expected of them, it's up to you to keep the people in order."

"Or I will be killed," Kirk said.

"Precisely. I see that you too understand me very well."

Once in the street, Kirk glanced about quickly. Nobody was within earshot, or seemed to be following them. He said quietly to Spock:

"That mind-sifter of theirs must not be quite the terror they think it is."

"I advise you not to underestimate it, Captain," Spock said. "I was able to resist it, partly with a little Vulcan discipline, partly by misdirection. But on the next higher setting, I am sure I would have been unable to protect myself."

"And I wouldn't last even that long. The question is now, how do we persuade these Organians to resist? To strike back, knock the Klingons off balance, maybe until the Federation fleet gets here?"

"Verbal persuasion seems to be ineffective," Spock said. "Perhaps a more direct approach?"

"My thought exactly. Didn't I see something that looked like a munitions dump near the citadel? I thought so. All right, let's try a little direct communication."

"The suggestion has merit. Would tonight do?"

"If you have no previous engagement," Kirk said. "Of course, we're short of tools."

"I am sure," Spock said, "the Klingons will provide whatever is necessary."

"It's a pleasure doing business with you, Mr. Spock."

The guards at the munitions depot were tough and highly trained, but nothing they had yet encountered on Organia had prepared them for anyone like Kirk and Spock. Two of them went quietly to sleep on duty within a few seconds of each other, were relieved of their phasers and locked in an empty storeroom, lovingly cocooned in baling wire.

Inside the dump, Kirk located a crate that seemed to contain some form of chemical explosive. He opened it. A few moments later, Spock appeared from the shadows.

"I have one of their sonic grenades," he murmured, "and I have improvised a delayed-action fuse. The combination should provide a most satisfactory display."

"Good. Fire away."

Spock made a pulling gesture, carefully tucked the grenade inside the crate, and ran, Kirk at his heels.

Three minutes later, the night lit up. Giant explosions rocked it, followed by strings of subsidiary explosions. Missiles flew in all directions. An immense cloud formed over the city, its underside flickering with the fires and detonations below it.

"You were right, Mr. Spock," Kirk said when the clamor had begun to die down. "A most satisfactory display. I only hope that the council draws the moral. Obviously they can't fight the Klingons directly, but they could make Organia useless to them."

"In the meantime," Spock said. "I earnestly suggest that we find ourselves a deep, deep hole, Captain. Somehow I cannot think that Commander Kor will believe the Organians did this."

"Nor do I. Let's vanish."

Perhaps one or both of them should have anticipated Kor's next move. Two hours later, in an empty, lightless hut near the outskirts of the village, they heard a distant, buzzing whine from the direction of the citadel.

"Phasers," Spock said.

"Yes, Klingon phasers—a lot of them, all being fired at once. Odd. It doesn't sound at all like a battle, or even a riot."

The answer came rumbling down the street outside within another hour, in the form of an armored vehicle. From a loudspeaker atop it, a recorded voice was bellowing:

"This is the military governor. In the courtyard of my headquarters, two hundred Organian hostages have just been killed. In two hours more, two hundred more will die, and two hundred more after that—until the two Federation spies are turned over to us. The blood of the hostages is on your hands. The executions will be carried on until the saboteurs are surrendered. This is the order of Kor. Attention, all subjects! This is the military governor. In the courtyard of my headquarters . . ."

Kirk and Spock were silent for a long time after the lumbering vehicle had become inaudible. At last Kirk whispered, appalled: "That tears it."

"Yes, Captain. And the Organians no more know where we are than Kor does. We must give ourselves up, and speedily."

"Wait a minute. Let me think."

"But all those lives . . ."

"I know, I know. We've got to turn ourselves in. But

we've still got sidearms. Just possibly, we can force Kor to call the killings off."

"Unlikely, Captain," Spock said. "Commander Kor may be a mass murderer, but he is clearly also a soldier."

"In that case, we'll just have to do as much damage as we can and keep them busy until the fleet shows up. The Federation invested a lot of money in our training, Mr. Spock. I think they're about due for a small return."

Spock estimated the odds against making it all the way to Kor's office at "approximately" 7,824.7 to one; but surprise and the phasers—set to heavy stun force—both told in their favor. When they reached the door of Kor's office, it was open, and no alarm had sounded. They could see the commander inside, seated at his desk, hands over his face, brooding. It seemed almost possible that he did not relish butchering unarmed civilians. When he looked up and saw Spock and Kirk before him, phasers leveled, a look of interest and appreciation appeared on his face.

"Just stay seated, Commander," Kirk said. "Mr. Spock, cover the door."

"You have done well to get this far, through my guards."

"I am afraid," Spock said, "that many of them are no longer in perfect operating condition."

"The fortunes of war. What next?"

"We're here. Call off your executions."

"You have not surrendered," Kor said in a reasonable tone of voice. "Drop your weapons and I will call off the executions. Otherwise you have accomplished nothing."

"We can certainly kill you," Kirk said grimly. "You're the Klingon governor. That might put quite a crimp in your operations."

"Don't be hasty," Kor said. "You will be interested in knowing that a Federation fleet is due here within the hour. Our fleet is prepared to meet them. Shall we wait and see the results before you pull the trigger?"

"I don't plan to pull it at all unless you force me to."

"Sheer sentimentality—or at best, mercy. A useless emotion in wartime. It is not a Klingon weakness." Kor smiled. "Think of it. While we talk here, in space above us the destiny of the galaxy will be decided for the next ten thousand years. May I offer you a drink? We can toast the victory of the Klingon fleet."

"I would suggest that you are premature," Spock said. "There are many possibilities."

"Commander," Kirk added, "we once had a nation on Earth called the Spartans—the finest warriors who ever walked our planet. They had their hour of conquest—but it was their chief opponent, Athens, who survived. Sparta knew only the arts of war. Athens was known as the mother of all the arts."

"A consoling analogy, but I think a little out of date," Kor said. "True, there is always some element of chance in a major war. Today we conquer; someday we may be defeated. But I am inclined to doubt it."

He rose. The phaser in Kirk's hand did not waver by a millimeter. Kor ignored it.

"Do you know why we are so strong?" Kor said. "Because we are a unit. Each of us is part of the greater whole. Always under surveillance. Even a commander like myself, always under surveillance, Captain. As you will note."

He waved toward the ceiling, smiling. Kirk did not look up.

"No doubt there's a scanner up there. However, Mr. Spock has the door covered, and I have you. At the first disturbance, I fire."

There was something remarkably like a yelp of dismay from Spock, and then the unmistakable sound of a phaser hitting the stone floor. Kirk whirled, trying to keep Kor simultaneously in the corner of his eye. At the same instant the door, which Spock had closed, burst open again and two Klingon soldiers charged in.

Kirk pulled the trigger. The phaser did not fire. Instead, it turned red hot in his hand. Instinctively, he threw it from him.

"Shoot!" Kor shouted. "Shoot, you blockheads!"

There were at least five soldiers in the room now, but one after another they too dropped their weapons, which lay glowing quietly against the stone. After a moment of dismay, the guards charged. Kirk set himself and swung.

He could feel the flesh of his fist sear as it hit. A Klingon grabbed him from behind—then let go with a howl.

"Their *bodies* are hot!" one of the soldiers gasped. He

was almost drowned out by a roar from the commander, who had tried to pick up a paper knife.

After that, for an eternal ten seconds, the enemies simply glared at each other incredulously. There was no sound but that of heavy breathing.

Then Ayelborne and Claymare came in. They were wearing their eternal smiles, which even Kirk had come to loathe.

"We are terribly sorry that we have been forced to interfere, gentlemen," Ayelborne said. "But we could not permit you to harm one another. There has been enough violence already."

"What are you talking about, you sheep?"

"We have put a stop to your brawling," Claymare said. "That is all."

"Let me get this straight," Kirk said slowly. "*You* put a stop to it? You? You mean you're going to slap our wrists?"

"Please, Captain," Claymare said. "You already know the answer. Not only your guns, but all instruments of destruction on this planet now have a potential surface temperature of three hundred and fifty degrees. Simple intent to use one renders it inoperative."

"My fleet . . ." Kor said.

"The same conditions exist upon both the opposing Starfleets," said Ayelborne. "There will be no battle."

"Ridiculous," Kor growled.

"I suggest you contact them. You too, Captain. Your ship is now within range of your communications device."

Kirk took out his communicator. "Kirk to *Enterprise*. Come in."

"Captain! Is that you?"

"Kirk here—report, Mr. Sulu."

"I don't know what to report, sir," Sulu's voice said. "We were just closing with the Klingon fleet when every control in the ship became too hot to handle. All except the communications board. If this is some new Klingon weapon, why didn't it disable that too?"

"I don't know," Kirk said heavily. "Stand by, Mr. Sulu. Ayelborne, how did you manage this?"

"I could not explain it to you with any hope of being understood, Captain. Suffice it to say that as I stand here, I also stand upon the bridge of your ship, upon the bridge

52

of every ship, upon the home planet of the Klingon Empire, on the home planet of your Federation. Some of my energies I share with your weapons—I and the rest of my people. We are putting a stop to this insane war."

"How dare you?" Kor shouted.

"You can't just stop our fleet," Kirk said, equally angrily. "You've got no right . . ."

"What happens in space is none of your business . . ."

"It is being stopped," Ayelborne said. "Unless both sides agree to an immediate cessation of hostilities, all your armed forces, wherever they may be, will be totally disabled."

"We have legitimate grievances against the Klingons," Kirk said. "They've invaded our territory, killed our citizens . . ."

"The disputed areas are not your territory," Kor raged. "You were trying to hem us in, cut off vital supplies, strangle our trade."

"Look here," Kirk said to the Organians, fighting himself back to some semblance of control. "We didn't ask you to intervene, but you should be the first to side with us now. The two hundred hostages who were killed . . ."

"No one has died, Captain," Claymare said calmly. "No one has died here for uncounted thousands of years. Nor do we mean that anyone shall."

"Let me ask you, Captain, what it is that you are defending," Ayelborne added, gently, as if amused. "Is it the right to wage war? To kill millions of innocent people? To destroy life on a planetary scale? Is that the 'right' you refer to?"

"Well, I . . ." Kirk said, and stopped. "Of course, nobody wants war, but sometimes you have to fight. Eventually, I suppose, we . . ."

"Yes, eventually you would make peace," Ayelborne said. "But only after millions had died. We are bringing it about now. The fact is, in the future you and the Klingons will become fast friends. You will work together in great harmony."

"Nonsense!" Kor said. Kirk realized that he had been standing shoulder to shoulder with the Klingon and moved away hastily.

"Of course, you are most discordant now," Ayelborne

said. "In fact, you will have to leave. The mere presence of beings like yourselves is acutely painful to us."

"What do you mean?" Kirk said. "You don't differ significantly from us, no matter what tricks you've mastered."

"Once we did not differ significantly," Claymare said. "But that was millions of years ago. Now we have developed beyond the need for physical bodies at all. This appearance is only for your convenience. Now we shall put it off."

"Hypnosis!" Kor cried. "Captain, those weapons may never have been hot at all! Grab them!"

Ayelborne and Claymare only smiled, and then they began to change. At first it was only a glow, becoming brighter and brighter, until they looked like metal statues in a furnace. Then the human shape faded. It was as if there were two suns in the room.

Kirk shut his eyes and covered them with both arms. He could still see the light. Finally, however, it began to fade.

The Organians were gone.

"Fascinating," Spock said. "Pure thought—or pure energy? In any event, totally incorporeal. Not life as we know it at all."

"But the planet," Kirk said. "The buildings—this citadel . . ."

"Probably the planet is real enough. But the rest, conventionalizations, no doubt, just as they said. Useless to them—points of reference for us. I should guess that they are as far above us on the evolutionary scale as we are above the amoeba."

There was a long silence. Finally, Kirk turned toward Kor.

"Well, Commander," he said, "I guess that takes care of the war. Since the Organians aren't going to let us fight, we might as well get started on being friends."

"Yes," Kor said. He thrust out his hand. "Still, in a way, Captain, it's all rather saddening."

"Saddening? Because they're so much more advanced than we are? But it took millions of years. Even the gods didn't spring into being overnight."

"No, that doesn't sadden me," Kor said. "I'm only sorry that they wouldn't let us fight." He sighed. "It would have been glorious."

COURT MARTIAL
(Don M. Mankiewicz and Steven W. Carabatsos)

The *Enterprise* weathered the ion storm somehow, but one man was dead, and damage to the ship was considerable. Kirk was forced to order a nonscheduled layover for repairs at Star Base 11, a huge complex serving the dual role of graving dock and galactic command outpost.

He made a full report to the portmaster, Senior Captain Stone, a craggy Negro who had once been a flight officer himself; Kirk had known him in those days, though not well. The report, of course, had to include an affidavit in the matter of Records Officer Benjamin Finney, deceased, and Kirk turned that in last and only after long study. Stone noticed his hesitation, but was patient. At last he said, "That makes three times you've read it, Captain. Is there an error?"

"No," Kirk said, "but the death of a crewman . . . When you have to sign these affidavits, you relive the moment." He signed the paper and passed it to Stone.

"I know. But you can't fight Regulations. Now, let's see; the extract from your ship's computer log, confirming the deposition?"

"In the other folder."

"Good . . . though it's a great pity too. The service can't afford to lose men like Officer Finney. If he'd only gotten out of the pod in time . . ."

"I waited until the last possible moment," Kirk said. "The storm got worse. We were on double-red alert. I had to jettison."

The office door swung open suddenly. A young woman was standing there—young, and pretty, but obviously under great stress. She glared wildly at Kirk, who recognized her instantly.

"There you are!" she cried. "I wanted one more good look at you!"

"Jame!"

"Yes, Jame! And you're the man who killed my father!"

"Do you really think that?" Kirk said.

"More than that! I think you deliberately murdered him!"

"Jame, Jame, stop and think what you're saying." Kirk stepped toward her. "We were friends, you know that. I would no more have hurt your father than I'd hurt you."

"Friends! That's a lie! You never were! You hated him, all your life! And you finally killed him!"

Stone, who had been discreetly pretending to study the documents, rose suddenly and moved between them. Jame was obviously fighting back a storm of tears. Kirk watched her in dismay.

"Captain Kirk," Stone said in a voice as hard as his name, "you say you jettisoned the pod *after* the double-red alert?"

"You have my sworn deposition," Kirk said.

"Then, Captain, it is my duty to presume you have committed willful perjury. According to the extract from your computer log, you jettisoned the pod *before* the double-red alert. Consider yourself relieved of command. A board of inquiry will determine whether a general court martial is in order."

Kirk never saw the board. As far as he was concerned, the inquiry consisted of Portmaster Stone and a recorder, which was to produce the tape the board would study.

"Where do you want me to begin?" Kirk said.

Stone pushed a cup of coffee toward Kirk. "Tell me about Officer Finney."

"We'd known each other a long time. He was an instructor at the Academy when I was a midshipman. But that didn't stop us from beginning a close friendship. His daughter, Jame, the girl who was in your office last night, was named after me."

"The friendship—it rather cooled with the years, didn't it? No, please speak, Captain, the recorder can't see you nodding."

"Yes, it did. I relieved him on watch once, on the USS *Republic*, and found the vent circuit to the fusion chamber open. If we'd gone under fusion power, the ship would have blown. As it was, it was contaminating the air of the engine room. I closed the switch and logged the error. He drew a reprimand and went to the bottom of the promotion list."

"And he blamed you for that?"

"Yes. He'd been kept on at the Academy as an instructor for an unusually long time. As a result, he was late being assigned to a starship. He felt the delay looked bad on his record. My action, he believed, made things worse. However, I couldn't very well have let an oversight of that magnitude go unreported."

"Comment by examining officer: Service record of Officer Finney to be appended to this transcript. Now, Captain, let's get to the specifics of the storm."

"Weatherscan indicated an ion storm dead ahead," Kirk said. "I sent Finney into the pod." For the benefit of possible civilians on the board, Kirk added, "The pod is outside the ship, attached to the skin. One of our missions is to get radiation readings in abnormal conditions, including ion storms. This can only be done by direct exposure of the necessary instruments in a plastic pod. However, in a major storm the pod rapidly picks up a charge of its own that becomes a danger to the rest of the ship, and we have to get rid of it."

"Why Finney? If he blamed you . . ."

"He may have blamed me because he never rose to command rank. But I don't assign jobs on the basis of who blames me, but whose name is on top of the duty roster. It was Finney's turn. He had just checked in with me when we hit the leading edge of the storm. Not bad at first. Then we began encountering field-variance, force two. The works. I finally signaled a double-red alert. Finney knew he had only a matter of seconds. I gave him those seconds, and more—but it wasn't enough. I can't explain his not getting out. He had the training, he had the reflexes, and he had plenty of time."

"Then why, Captain," Stone said, "does the computer log—yours, made automatically at the time—indicate that there was no double-red alert when you jettisoned?"

"I don't know," Kirk said.

"Could the computer be wrong?"

"Mr. Spock, my first officer, is running a survey now," Kirk said grimly. "But the odds are next to impossible."

Stone looked at Kirk long and penetratingly, and then reached out and shut off the recorder. "I'm not supposed to do this," he said. "But—look, Kirk. Not one man in a million can do what you and I did: serve as a starship captain. A hundred decisions a day, hundreds of lives staked on every one of them being right. You've been out nineteen months on this last mission. You've taken no furlough, had virtually no rest in all that time. You're played out—exhausted."

Kirk was beginning to get the drift of this, and he did not like it. "That's the way you see it?"

"That's the way my report will read," Stone said, "if you cooperate."

"Physical breakdown," Kirk said. "Possibly even mental collapse."

"Well . . . yes."

"I'd be admitting that a man died because . . ."

"Admit nothing," Stone said. "Let me bury the matter, here and now. No starship captain has ever stood trial before. I don't want you to be the first."

"But what if I'm guilty?" Kirk said steadily. "Shouldn't I be punished?"

"I'm thinking of the service, dammit! I won't have it smeared by . . ."

"By what, Portmaster?"

"All right!" Stone said explosively. "By an evident perjurer who's covering up bad judgment, cowardice, or something even worse!"

"That's as far as you go, Captain," Kirk said, instantly on his feet, "or I'll forget you *are* a captain. I'm telling you, I was on that bridge. I know what happened. I know what I did."

"It's in the transcript," Stone said, equally hotly, "and computer transcripts don't lie. You decide, Captain. Bury the matter and accept a ground assignment—or demand a general court, and bring down on your head the full disciplinary powers of Star Fleet."

"I have already decided," Kirk said. "Turn the recorder back on."

The courtroom was stark. There was one main viewing screen, a recorder, a witness chair, one table each for prosecution and defense, and a high bench where sat Portmaster Stone and the three members of the court-martial board. The prosecutor was a cool, lovely blonde woman named Areel Shaw, who as it happened was an old friend of Kirk's. ("All my old friends look like doctors," Bones McCoy had commented, "and all Jim's old friends look like her.") It was on her advice that Kirk had retained Samuel T. Cogley, a spry old eccentric who put his trust not in computers, but in books. He did not inspire much confidence, though Kirk was convinced that Areel had meant well.

Stone called the court to order by striking an ancient naval ship's bell. "I declare that the General Court of Star Base Eleven is now in session. Captain James T. Kirk will rise. Charge: culpable negligence. Specification: in that, on Star Date 2947.3, by such negligence, you did cause loss of life, to wit, the life of Records Officer Benjamin Finney. Charge: conduct prejudicial to the good order of the service. Specification: in that, thereafter, you failed accurately to report the same incident in your captain's log. To these charges and specifications, how do you plead?"

"Not guilty," Kirk said quietly.

"I have appointed, as members of this court, Space Command Representative Chandra and Star Command Captains Li Chow and Krasnowsky. I direct your attention to the fact that you have a right to ask for substitute officers if you feel that any of these named harbor prejudice harmful to your case."

"I have no objections, sir."

"And do you consent to the service of Lieutenant Shaw as prosecuting officer, and to my own service as chief judge?"

"Yes, sir."

"Lieutenant Shaw," Stone said, "you may proceed."

Areel Shaw stepped into the arena. "I call Mr. Spock."

Spock took the stand and passed to the recorder attendant his identity disk. The recorder promptly said: "Spock, S-179-276-SP. Service rank: commander. Position: first officer, science officer. Current assignment: USS *Enterprise*. Commendations: Vulcan scientific Legion of Honor. Awards of valor: twice decorated by Galactic Command."

"Mr. Spock," Areel Shaw said, "as a science officer, you know a great deal about computers, don't you?"

"I know all about them," Spock said levelly.

"Do you know of any possible malfunction that would cause one to recall an event inaccurately?"

"No."

"Or any malfunction that *has* caused an inaccuracy in *this* one?"

"No. Nevertheless, it is inaccurate."

"Please explain."

"It reports," Spock said, "that the jettison button was pressed before the double-red alert—in other words, that Captain Kirk was reacting to an emergency that did not then exist. That is not only illogical, but impossible."

"Were you watching him the exact moment he pressed the button?"

"No. I was occupied. We were already at red-alert."

"Then how can you dispute the record of the log?"

"I do not dispute it," Spock said. "I merely state it to be wrong. I know the captain. He would not . . ."

"Captain Stone," Areel Shaw said, "please instruct the witness not to speculate."

"Sir," Spock said to Stone, "I am half Vulcan. Vulcans do not speculate. I speak from pure logic. If I let go of a hammer on a high-gravity planet, I do not need to see it fall to know that it has fallen. Human beings have characteristics that determine their behavior just as inanimate objects do. I say it is illogical for Captain Kirk to have reacted to an emergency that did not exist, and impossible for him to act out of panic or malice. That is not his nature."

"In your opinion," Areel Shaw said.

"Yes," Spock said with obvious reluctance. "In my opinion."

The personnel officer of the *Enterprise* was called next. "With reference to Records Officer Finney," Areel asked him, "was there, in his service record, a report of disciplinary action for failure to close a circuit?"

"Yes, ma'am," the P.O. said.

"This charge was based upon a log entry by the officer who relieved him. Who was that officer?"

"Ensign James T. Kirk," the P.O. said softly.

"Speak louder, for the recorder, please. That is now the Captain Kirk who sits in this courtroom?"

"Yes, ma'am."

"Thank you. Your witness, Mr. Cogley."

"No questions," Cogley said.

Areel next called Bones McCoy to the stand, and went after him with cool efficiency. "Doctor, you are, on the record, an expert in psychology, especially in space psychology—patterns that develop in the close quarters of a ship during long voyages in deep space."

"I know something about it."

"Your academic record, and your experience, doctor, belie your modesty. Is it possible that Officer Finney blamed the defendant for the incident we have just heard your personnel officer describe—blamed him and hated him for being passed over for promotion, blamed him for never having been given a command of his own, hated him for having to serve under him?"

"Of course, it's possible," McCoy said.

"Then, isn't it also possible that all that hatred, directed against Captain Kirk, could have caused a like response in the captain?"

"You keep asking what's possible," McCoy said. "To the human mind almost anything is possible. The fact, however, is that I have never observed such an attitude in Captain Kirk."

"What about an attitude generated in his subconscious mind?"

"I object!" Sam Cogley said. "Counsel is leading the witness into making unprovable subjective speculations."

"On the contrary, your honor," Areel said. "I am asking a known expert in psychology for an expert psychological opinion."

"Objection overruled," Stone said. "You may proceed."

"Captain Kirk, then," Areel said relentlessly, "could have become prejudiced against Officer Finney without having been aware of it—prejudiced in such a way that his judgment became warped. Is that *theoretically* possible, doctor?"

"Yes," McCoy said, "it's possible. But highly unlikely."

"Thank you. Your witness, Mr. Cogley."

"No questions."

"Then I call James T. Kirk."

When Kirk's identity disc was placed in the recorder, the machine said: "Kirk, SC-937-0176-CEC. Service rank: captain. Position: starship command. Current assignment: USS *Enterprise*. Commendations: Palm leaf of Axanar peace mission. Grankite order of tactics, class of excellence. Pentares ribbon of commendation, classes first and second . . ."

"May it please the court," Areel Shaw said. The recorder attendant shut off the machine. "The prosecution concedes the inestimable record of Captain Kirk, and asks consent that it be entered as if read."

"Mr. Cogley," Stone said, "do you so consent?"

Cogley smiled disarmingly, stretched a bit in his chair, and rose. "Well, sir," he said, "I wouldn't want to be the one to slow the wheels of progress. On the other hand, I wouldn't want those wheels to run over my client in their unbridled haste. May I point out, sir, that this is a *man* we are examining, so perhaps a little longer look would not be amiss. The court's convenience is important, but his *rights* are paramount."

"Continue," Stone told the recorder attendant. The machine said:

"Awards of valor: Medal of Honor, silver palm with cluster. Three times wounded, honor roll. Galactic citation for conspicuous gallantry. Karagite Order of Heroism . . ."

It took quite a long time, during which Areel Shaw looked at the floor. Kirk could not tell whether she was fuming at having been outmaneuvered, or was simply ashamed of the transparency of her trick. Doubtless she did not want the court to be able to tell, either.

"Now, Captain. Despite the record, you continue to maintain that there was a double-red alert before you jettisoned the pod?"

"Yes, ma'am. There was."

"And you cannot explain why the computer record shows otherwise."

"No, I cannot."

"And in fact you'd do it again under the same circumstances."

"Objection!" Cogley said. "Counsel is now asking the witness to convict himself in advance of something he hasn't done yet and, we maintain, didn't do in the past!"

"It's all right, Sam," Kirk said. "I'm willing to answer. Lieutenant Shaw, I have been trained to command. The training doesn't sharpen a man's verbal skills. But it does sharpen his sense of duty—and confidence in himself to discharge that duty."

"May it please the court," Areel Shaw said, "I submit that the witness is not being responsive."

"He's answering the question," Stone said, "and he has a right to explain his answers. Proceed, Captain Kirk."

"Thank you, sir. We were in the worst kind of ion storm. And I was in command. I made a judgment—a command judgment. And because it was necessary to make that judgment, a man died. But the lives of my entire crew and my ship were in danger, and *not* to have made that judgment, to wait, to have been indecisive when it was time to act, would in my mind have been criminal. I did not act out of panic, or malice. I did what I was duty-bound to do. And of course, Lieutenant Shaw, I would do it again; that is the responsibility of command."

There was a brief hush. Areel Shaw broke it at last, turning to Stone.

"Your honor, the prosecution does not wish to dishonor this man. But I must invite the court's attention now to the visual playback of the log extract of the *Enterprise*'s computer."

"It is so ordered."

The main viewing screen lit up. When it was over, Areel Shaw said, almost sadly, "If the court will notice the scene upon which we froze, the screen plainly shows the defendant's finger pressing the jettison button. The condition signal reads RED-ALERT. Not double red—but simply red. When the pod containing Officer Finney was jettisoned, the emergency did not as yet exist.

"The prosecution rests."

Thunderstruck, Kirk stared at the screen. He had just seen the impossible.

During the recess, Sam Cogley calmly leafed through legal books in the room assigned to them, while Kirk paced the floor in anger and frustration.

"I know what I did!" Kirk said. "That computer report is an outright impossibility."

"Computers don't lie," Cogley said.

"Sam, are you suggesting *I* did?"

"I'm suggesting that maybe you did have a lapse. It's

possible, with the strain you were under. Jim, there's still time to change our plea. I could get you off."

"Two days ago, I would have staked my life on my judgment."

"You did. Your professional life."

"I know what I did," Kirk said, spacing each word. "But if you want to pull out . . ."

"There's nowhere to go," Cogley said. "Except back into court in half an hour. The verdict's a foregone conclusion, unless we change our plea."

Kirk's communicator beeped and he took it out. "Kirk here."

"Captain," Spock's voice said, "I have run a full survey on the computer."

"I'll tell you what you found," Kirk said. "Nothing."

"You sound bitter."

"Yes, Mr. Spock. I am. But not so bitter as to fail to thank you for your efforts."

"My duty, Captain. Further instructions?" There actually seemed to be emotion in Spock's voice, but if he felt any such stirring, he was unable to formulate it.

"No. I'm afraid you'll have to find yourself a new chess partner, Mr. Spock. Over and out."

Cogley gathered up an armful of books and started for the door. "I've got to go to a conference in chambers with Stone and Shaw."

"Look," Kirk said. "What I said before—I was a little worked up. You did the best you could."

Cogley nodded and opened the door. Behind it, her arm raised to knock, was Jame Finney.

"Jame!" Kirk said. "Sam, this is Officer Finney's daughter."

"A pleasure," Cogley said.

"Mr. Cogley," she said, "you have to stop this. Make him change his plea. Or something. Anything. I'll help if I can."

Sam Cogley looked slightly perplexed, but he said only, "I've tried."

"It's too late for anything like that, Jame," Kirk said. "But I appreciate your concern."

"It can't be too late. Mr. Cogley, my father's dead. Ruining Jim won't bring him back."

"That's a commendable attitude, Miss Finney," Cogley

said. "But a little unusual, isn't it? After all, Captain Kirk is accused of *causing* your father's death."

"I was . . ." Jame said, and stopped. She seemed suddenly nervous. "I was just thinking of Jim."

"Thank you, Jame," Kirk said. "But I'm afraid we've had it. You'd better go."

When the door closed, Cogley put his books down. "How well do you know that girl?" he said.

"Since she was a child."

"Hmm. I suppose that might explain her attitude. Curious, though. Children don't usually take such a dispassionate view of the death of a parent."

"Oh, she didn't at first. She was out for my blood. Almost hysterical. Charged into Stone's office calling me a murderer."

"Why didn't you tell me that before?"

"Why," Kirk said, "the subject never came up. Is it important?"

"I don't know," Cogley said thoughtfully. "It's—a false note, that's all. I don't see what use we could put it to now."

Stone rang the court to order. He had hardly done so when Spock and McCoy materialized squarely in the midst of the room—a hair-raisingly precise piece of transporter work. They moved directly to Kirk and Cogley; the latter stood and Spock whispered to him urgently.

"Mr. Cogley," Stone said harshly, "what's the meaning of this display?"

"May it please the court," Mr. Cogley said, "we mean no disrespect, but these officers have unearthed new evidence, and they could conceive of no way to get it to the court in time but by this method."

"The counsel for the defense," Areel Shaw said, "has already rested his case. Mr. Cogley is well-known for his theatrics . . ."

"Is saving an innocent man's life a theatric?" He turned to Stone. "Sir, my client has been deprived of one of his most important rights in this trial—the right to be confronted by the witnesses against him. *All* the witnesses, your honor. And the most devastating witness against my client is not a human being, but an information system—a machine."

"The excerpt from the computer log has been shown."

"Your honor, a log excerpt is not the same as the machine that produced it. I ask that this court adjourn and reconvene on board the *Enterprise* itself."

"I object, your honor," Areel Shaw said. "He's trying to turn this into a circus."

"Yes!" Cogley said. "A circus! Do you know what the first circus was, Lieutenant Shaw? An arena, where men met danger face to face, and lived or died. This is indeed a circus. In this arena, Captain Kirk will live or die, for if you take away his command he will be a dead man. But he has not met his danger face to face. He has the right to confront his accuser, and it matters nothing that his accuser is a machine. If you do not grant him that right, you have not only placed us on a level with the machine —you have elevated the machine above us! Unless I am to move for a mistrial, I ask that my motion be granted. But more than that, gentlemen: In the name of humanity fading in the shadow of the machine, I demand it. I demand it!"

The members of the board put their heads together. At last Stone said: "Granted."

"Mr. Spock," Cogley said. "How many chess games did you play with the computer during recess?"

"Five."

"And the outcome?"

"I won them all."

"May that be considered unusual, Mr. Spock, and if so, why?"

"Because I myself programed the computer to play chess. It knows my game; and as has been observed before, it cannot make an error. Hence, even if I myself never make an error, the best I can hope to achieve against it is a stalemate. I have been able to win against Captain Kirk now and then, but against the computer, never—until now. It therefore follows that someone has adjusted either the chess programing or the memory banks. The latter would be the easier task."

"I put it to you, Mr. Spock, that even the latter would be beyond the capacity of most men, isn't that so? Well, then, what men, aboard ship, would it *not* be beyond?"

"The captain, myself—and the Records Officer."

"Thank you, you may step down. I now call Captain Kirk. Captain, describe what steps you took to find Officer Finney after the storm."

"When he did not respond to my call," Kirk said, "I ordered a phase-one search for him. Such a search assumes that its object is injured and unable to respond to the search party."

"It also presupposes that the man *wishes to be found?*"

"Of course, Sam."

"Quite. Now, with the court's permission, although Mr. Spock is now in charge of this ship, I am going to ask Captain Kirk to describe what Mr. Spock has done, to save time, which you will see in a moment is a vital consideration. May I proceed?"

"Well . . . . All right."

"Captain?"

"Mr. Spock has ordered everybody but the members of this court and the command crew to leave the ship. This includes the engine crew. Our impulse engines have been shut down and we are maintaining an orbit by momentum alone."

"And when the orbit begins to decay?" Stone said.

"We hope to be finished before that," Cogley said. "But that is the vital time element I mentioned. Captain, is there any other step Mr. Spock has taken?"

"Yes, he has rigged an auditory sensor to the log computer. In effect, it will now be able to hear—as will we—every sound occurring on this ship."

"Thank you. Dr. McCoy to the stand, please. Doctor, I see you have a small device with you. What is it, please?"

"It is a white-noise generator."

"I see. All right, Mr. Spock."

At the console, Spock turned a switch. The bridge at once shuddered to an intermittent pounding, like many drums being beaten.

"Could you reduce the volume a little?" Cogley said. "Thank you. Your honor, that sound is caused by the heartbeats of all the people in this room. With your permission, I am going to ask Dr. McCoy to take each person's pulse, and then use the white-noise device to mask those pulsebeats out, so they will be eliminated from the noise we are hearing."

"What is the purpose of this rigmarole, your honor?" Areel Shaw demanded.

"I think you suspect that as well as I do, Lieutenant," Stone said. "Proceed, Dr. McCoy."

As Bones moved from person to person, the eerie multiple thumping became simpler, softer.

"That's all," McCoy said.

No one breathed. Faintly, somewhere, one beat still sounded.

"May it please the court," Cogley said quietly, "the remaining pulse you hear, I think we will shortly find, is that of Officer Finney. Mr. Spock, can you localize it?"

"B deck, between sections 18Y and 27D. I have already sealed off that section."

Kirk hesitated, then came to a decision. "Captain Stone," he said, "this is my problem. I would appreciate it if no one would leave the bridge."

As he turned to leave, Spock handed him a phaser. "The weapons room is within those quadrants, sir," he said quietly. "He may be armed. This is already set on stun."

"Thank you, Mr. Spock."

He moved cautiously down the corridor in the sealed section, calling at intervals:

"All right, Ben. It's all over. Ben! Officer Finney!"

For a while there was no answer. Then, suddenly, a figure stepped out of a shadow, phaser leveled.

"Hello, Captain," Officer Finney said.

Kirk found that he could not answer. Though he had been sure that this was the solution, the emotional impact of actually being face to face with the "dead" man was unexpectedly powerful. Finney smiled a hard smile.

"Nothing to say, Captain?"

"Yes," Kirk said. "I'm glad to see you alive."

"You mean you're relieved because your precious career is saved. Well, you're wrong. You've just made things worse for everyone."

"Put the phaser down, Ben. Why go on with it?"

"You wouldn't leave it alone," Finney said. "You've taken away my choices. Officers and gentlemen, com-

68

manders all . . . except for Finney and his one mistake. A long time ago, but they don't forget. No, they never forget."

"Ben, I logged that mistake of yours. Blame me, not them."

"But they're to blame," Finney said. "All of them. I was a good officer. I really was. I loved the service like no man ever did."

Slowly, Kirk began to move in on him.

"Stand back, Captain. No more—I warn you—"

"You're sick, Ben. We can help you—"

"One more step—"

Suddenly, Jame's voice cried down the corridor, "Father! *Father!*"

Finney's head jerked around. With a quick lunge, Kirk knocked the phaser from his hand. At the same moment, Jame appeared, rushing straight into the distraught man's arms.

"Jame!"

"It's all right, father," she said, moving her hand over the tortured officer's brow. "It's all right."

"Don't, Jame," he said. "You've got to understand. I had to do it . . . after what they did to me . . ."

"Excuse me," Kirk said. "But if we don't get this ship back under power, we'll all be dead."

"Mr. Cogley," Stone said, "while this trial is obviously not over yet, I think we must congratulate you and Mr. Spock and Dr. McCoy for a truly classical piece of detective work. Would you tell us, please, how the idea that Officer Finney was still alive even entered your head?"

"I began to suspect that, your honor, when Captain Kirk told me about the change of heart Officer Finney's daughter had had about the captain. If she knew he wasn't dead, she had no reason to blame the Captain for anything."

"But how could she know that?" Stone asked.

"She had been reading her father's papers. Perhaps she didn't know the facts, but the general tone of what he had written must have gotten through to her. A man suffering delusions of persecution wants to set down his complaints. She read them; she knew from childhood the kind of man the captain is; and she's fundamentally fair and decent."

He paused and looked soberly over toward Kirk.

"Or maybe," he said, "it was just instinct. Thank God, there's that much of the animal left in us. Whatever it was, the result is that she now has back both her father and her childhood friend."

"Her father," Stone said, "will also have to stand trial."

"I know that," Cogley said quietly. "I ask the court to appoint me his defense counsel. And off the record, your honor, I have the feeling I'll win."

"Off the record," Stone said, "I wouldn't be a bit surprised."

OPERATION—ANNIHILATE!

(Steven W. Carabatsos)

The spread of the insanity was slow, and apparently patternless, but it was also quite inexorable. The first modern instance in the record was Aldebaran Magnus Five. Then, Cygni Theta 12. Most recently, Ingraham B—recently enough so that the *Enterprise* had been able to get there within a year of the disaster.

Nothing had been learned from the mission. There were no apparent connections among the three planets—except that on each one, the colonists had gone totally, irrevocably mad, all at the same time, and had killed each other. It hadn't been warfare; the people had simply fallen upon each other in the streets, in their homes, everywhere, until there were none left.

It was Spock who had suggested that there would nevertheless be a pattern, if one assumed that the long-dead civilizations of the Orion complex had fallen to the same cause. The archeological evidence was ambiguous, and besides, the peoples of the cluster had not been human. There was no *a priori* reason why they should have been subject to the afflictions of human beings.

Nevertheless, given the assumption, the computer was able to plot a definite localization and rate of spread—like an amoeboid blotch upon the stars, thrusting out a pseudopod to another world at gradually shortening intervals. If the radioactive dating of the deaths of the Orion civilizations was correct, as it almost surely was—and if the assumption was correct, which was sheer speculation—then the madness had taken two hundred years to appear on its second victim-world, less than a century to crop up a third time, and the next outbreak was due within the next month.

"On Deneva, I would say," Spock added. "An Earth-type planet, colonized about a century ago. Pleasant climate, no hazardous life-forms. Of course, I could well be completely wrong about this, since my basic premise is completely *ad hoc*."

"Never mind the logical holes," Kirk said. "Mr. Sulu, lay in a course for Deneva. Warp factor four. Lieutenant Uhura, tell Starship Command where we're going and why. When we break into the Denevan system, raise the planet."

But there was no time for that. The first thing the sensors showed when the *Enterprise* emerged in that system was a Denevan ship apparently on its way toward throwing itself into the Denevan sun.

"Status!" Kirk said tensely.

"He's got a huge jump on us, Captain," Sulu said. "A one-man vessel—sub-light velocity but under heavy acceleration."

"Contact, Captain," Uhura said.

"Denevan ship, this is the USS *Enterprise!* Break your heading! You're on a collision course with your sun! Fire your retros!"

From the speaker came a faint and agonized voice. "Help me . . . please . . . help me . . ."

"We're trying to! Spock, can we reach him with a tractor beam?"

"No, sir," Spock said. "Too much solar magnetism."

"Sulu, intercept. Denevan, pull back! Fire your retros!"

"Help me, please . . . take it out . . . take it out . . . please . . ."

"Skin temperature four hundred degrees," Spock said. "Rising fast."

"He's too close, Captain," Sulu said. "He'll burn—and so will we if we keep this up."

"Keep closing."

"Skin temperature now eight hundred degrees," Spock said.

Suddenly the Denevan's voice came through again, much stronger, and much changed. It seemed almost jubilant. "I did it! It's gone! I'm free. I'm free! I won—oh great God, the sun, *the sun* . . ."

The words ended in a terrible scream.

"He's gone, Captain," Sulu reported.

"Vector!" Kirk shouted. Then, as the great ship shuddered into its emergency turn, he stared blindly at the now-silent speaker.

"What did he do that for?" he said. "Even if his instruments weren't working, we warned him."

"Obviously suicide," Spock said.

"But why? And Spock, I don't think he wanted to die. You heard him. He asked us to help him."

"Suicides are not rational," Spock said. "By definition."

"Mr. Spock, that may be perfectly good logic, but I'm afraid it doesn't satisfy me. And I hate puzzles. They don't look good on the log."

"Captain," Uhura said. "I've gotten through to Deneva itself."

"Good, let's hear it. Hello, Deneva, USS *Enterprise* calling."

"Enterprise, please hurry!" a strong voice cried promptly. There was a blast of static. "Help us! I don't have much time! They'll know!"

"Another madman?" Kirk said to nobody in particular. "Lieutenant, can't you clean up some of that static?"

"It's solar static, sir. Should clear gradually as we pull away."

"Hello, Deneva, *Enterprise* here. Please repeat."

"Hurry! Hurry! They'll know in a minute! We need help!"

There was more static. Kirk said: "We're on our way, Deneva. What's wrong? Please explain."

But there was no answer, only still more static. Uhura turned in her chair. "Contact broken, Captain. I'm trying to reestablish, but I think they've switched out."

"All right, Sulu. Course for Deneva—on the double."

The landing party—Kirk, Spock, McCoy, two security guards, and Yeoman Zahara—materialized in an empty city street. There were supposed to be more than a million colonists and their descendants on this planet, nearly a hundred thousand in this city alone; yet the place looked deserted.

"Where is everybody?" Kirk said.

Spock scanned in a circle with his tricorder. "They are here. But they are all indoors. Apparently just sitting there. There is a signal center in that building across the street. It is inoperative, but the power is up."

"All right, let's . . ."

"Party approaching," Spock interrupted. "Four people —make it five. Coming fast."

He had hardly spoken when five men came around the corner at top speed. They seemed to be ordinary civilians, but Kirk had the instant impression that their faces were warped with agony. All carried clubs. The instant they saw the group from the *Enterprise,* they burst into a bestial shrieking. It was impossible to tell which of them was screaming what.

"Run! Get away! We don't want to hurt you! Go back! Look out!"

"Fire to stun!" Kirk shouted. The Denevans charged, swinging their clubs.

"Go away! Please! They'll get you! No! Get away from here! We'll have to kill you . . ."

Kirk fired, followed by the others. The charging Denevans fell in a clatter of clubs. Kirk approached them cautiously. Despite the fact that they had just taken the heavy stun force of a phaser blast at close range, they seemed to be twitching slightly.

"Could you make out all that shouting, Mr. Spock?"

"Indeed. They seemed greatly concerned for our safety —so concerned that they wanted to brain us. This may not be *the* insanity, but . . ."

"But it'll do for now," Kirk said. "Bones, check them over."

McCoy checked the unconscious bodies quickly, then rose, shaking his head puzzledly. "Something decidedly odd," he said. "These people should be pretty close to being vegetables for the next few hours. But I'm getting high readings, as though their nervous systems were being violently stimulated even while they're . . ."

He was interrupted by a woman's scream. Kirk whirled. "Fan out!" he said. "That came from that signal center. Come on!"

The scream came again. Inside the building there was a dark lobby of some sort, and a closed door, which turned out to be locked. Kirk lunged against it.

"Open up!" he shouted. "We're from the *Enterprise.*"

"They're here!" the woman screamed. "They're here! Keep them away!" Over her voice there was a heavy buzzing sound, which seemed to be rising in pitch.

Kirk and the two guards hit the door together. It burst

inward. Here was the signal center, all right, but it looked shoddy, unused. An elderly man lay unconscious on the floor; across the room, a girl was desperately holding a panel of some sort over a ventilation outlet, fighting with all her strength. As the party broke in she staggered backward, dropping the panel, covering her face with her hands and sobbing wildly.

Kirk pointed to the old man while he took the girl in his arms. "It's all right. You're safe."

She screamed again and began to struggle.

"Bones, a hypo! I can't hold her."

McCoy already had his sprayjet out, and a moment later the girl too had collapsed. "The man's alive," he reported. "Some sort of seizure, or maybe just exhaustion. I'd better get them both up to the ship."

"Right. Mr. Spock, you heard her. She called out that *they* were here. Your guess?"

"Notice, Captain," Spock said. "Rags stuffed under the door. Pieces of board jammed across the windows. As if they were in a state of siege."

"But by what? There are no harmful life-forms on this planet. And our sensors didn't pick up anything that didn't belong here."

"I am baffled, Captain."

"Bones, beam up with those two people and bring them around. I'm going to have to ask some questions. Mr. Spock, we'll go outside and resume looking around. Zahara, are you recording all of this?"

"Of course, Captain."

As they emerged from the communications center, Kirk saw one of the security men standing near a sheltered, shadowy alleyway. He moved toward the party as it appeared.

"Anything, Abrams?"

"Yes sir, but don't ask me what. Something moving back in there. Making a buzzing sound."

Kirk looked around, and then up. All the windows above him seemed to be empty, but in one there was the face of a man. His expression was a terrible combination of agony, fear and desperate hope.

"You!" Kirk shouted at him. "I want to talk to you!"

The face contorted and vanished. Kirk grunted with

annoyance. "All right, Spock, Abrams, let's go see what's back in there."

Phasers ready, they moved cautiously into the darkened alley. Almost at once the buzzing noise got louder, and something about the size of a football flew through the air over their heads. Then another.

"Phasers on kill!" Kirk shouted. But for a moment there were no more. Then suddenly Spock pointed. Another such object clung to a wall. Kirk fired.

The beam hit the thing squarely. But it refused to vanish. It simply clung to the wall for a long moment, even under the full force of the beam, and finally slipped off and fell to the earth.

They closed in warily, but there seemed to be no more of the creatures back here. Spock took tricorder readings on the downed object, which seemed to be no more than a gelatinous mass, amorphous, colorless, as though somebody had dumped a jellyfish out of a bucket. Kirk stared at it incredulously.

"What is that?"

"It isn't anything," Spock said promptly. "Not only should it have been destroyed by the phaser blast, but it does not register on the tricorder."

"It's real enough all the same," Kirk said. "And it acted alive. Can we take it along, Spock?"

"I advise against it. We have no proper equipment, and it may well be toxic, corrosive—there are a dozen possibilities."

"Whatever they are, they seem to like these shadows," Kirk said. "Let's get out back into the light. We know where we can find them if we want them, anyhow."

As they retreated, the buzzing noise began again. The next instant, one of the objects shot past Kirk and hit Spock squarely in the back, knocking him off his feet. The thing clung to him. His hands tore uselessly at his back. Then, somehow, it was gone, and Spock was lying face down in the alley.

Kirk knelt beside him. "Spock! Are you all right? The thing's gone. Can you stand?"

Spock's hands were still clutching his back. As Kirk spoke, he rolled over, his entire face working with the effort to control himself. He got slowly to his knees. Then

76

his mouth opened, and pitching forward, he began to scream.

Spock was in sick bay under heavy sedation; thus far, McCoy had been unable to think of anything else to do for him. In the interim, however, he had managed to revive the elderly man and the girl the landing party had found in the signal room on Deneva. The girl's name was Aurelan, the man's Menen. They did their best to answer Kirk's questions, but he found their answers difficult to comprehend.

"I know it must sound insane, Captain," Aurelan said, "but it's quite true."

Kirk shot a look at Zahara, who was recording. "You mean these things, whatever they are, have taken over the entire planet?"

"Except for ourselves," Menen said.

"There are over a million inhabitants of Deneva."

"There are millions of *them*," Menen said.

"When did they get to Deneva? How?"

"About four months ago," Menen said with some difficulty, "in a spaceship. We don't know any more than that. They didn't give us the time."

"It's a nightmare, Captain," Aurelan said. "Worse than a nightmare."

"The things don't communicate with you?"

"Oh, they communicate all right," Aurelan said bitterly. "Through pain. Once they attack you, something happens inside. We're not doctors, we don't know the details. But life is agony from then on."

Menen added, "My son told me—before he died—that they need bodies the way we need tools. Arms and legs —human beings. And once they take over, they can't be resisted. The people who tried to kill you in the street didn't want to hurt you. They wanted your help. But the things ordered them to attack you, and they had no choice."

"But why didn't they take you two over too?"

"We think they spared us so that we could maintain normal contacts with other planets and ships. They want ships, Captain. They need them. They're forcing our people to build ships right now."

"My brother, Noban . . ." Aurelan began.

"He's the man who flew his ship into the sun?"

Aurelan nodded sadly. "The creatures had him. He almost went mad from the pain. But he told us that Deneva is just a way-station for them. They mean to spread out. You see . . ." She paused and swallowed. "Their hosts become useless after a while. They go mad. And then the things need new hosts. More people. Planet after planet. They come, and they leave madness, and they go to the next . . ."

"In the name of God, Captain," Menen said, "you've got to do something!"

"I'll do what I can," Kirk said. "What about my first officer, Mr. Spock?"

"Is he important to your ship?" Aurelan said.

"Extremely," Kirk said. "And to me personally. He's one of my closest friends."

"In that case," Menen said, "kill him."

"What!"

"Kill him. Now. Quickly. Because only endless agony lies ahead for him, agony that will end in madness. If you are his friend, be merciful."

"Security calling Captain Kirk," said the bridge speaker.

"Kirk here."

"Captain, this is Ames. Mr. Spock has attacked his nurse and fled. He seems deranged."

"All decks security alert. He may be dangerous. Aurelan, Menen, you'd better get to your quarters and stay there."

They went quietly. Only seconds later, it seemed, the elevator door opened again and Spock charged out.

"Get away from the controls!" he screamed. "I have to take her down!"

Before anyone could move, he had reached the helm and had knocked Sulu down and away with one sweeping blow. The navigator and Scott leapt on him, but Spock was a powerful man; he sent them reeling.

"Security to the bridge!" Uhura was calling into her mike. "Alert! General alert to the bridge!"

Kirk joined in the melee, but they were all handicapped by the desire not to hurt Spock; the first officer had no such compunctions. They only barely managed to keep him away from the controls.

78

Then three security men appeared, and in a few moments Spock was held fast. "I have to take the ship down!" he panted. "I don't want to! Help me! Help me!"

Somehow McCoy was on the scene now, and elbowing his way through the crowd, he gave the first officer a shot. Spock collapsed at once.

"Get him back to sick bay," Kirk said, "and this time, strap him down."

The security men carried him out, with Kirk and McCoy following. It was a grim procession.

"Well, Menen warned me," Kirk said. "He told me that if Spock meant anything to me, I should kill him."

"Now *there's* a tomfool notion."

"Don't worry, Bones, the idea doesn't appeal to me either. But we've got to do something to help him."

"Well, I've at least gotten a start on it," McCoy said. "Come on in and I'll show you."

In McCoy's office, the surgeon showed Kirk a jar full of transparent liquid. In the fluid, a long, almost-transparent tendril drifted and twisted.

"It's a piece of living tissue of some sort," McCoy said. "Call it a tentacle. I took it out of Spock's spinal column an hour ago."

"Is that what causes the pain?"

McCoy nodded. "His entire nervous system has been infiltrated by this stuff. And far too thoroughly for conventional surgery to remove. I don't know how to get it out."

"Then if the old man is right," Kirk said, "this tissue is responsive to directives sent out by the other creatures."

"Or is it *the* creature?"

"Explain."

"By itself," McCoy said, "this stuff is just undifferentiated tissue. No organs. And I'd guess the same for the individual creatures we saw on the surface. They didn't look like things, but *parts* of things. Put them all together and—well, I'm sure they wouldn't spell 'Mother.' But that's about all I'm sure of."

"Do you know why it resists a phaser blast?"

"It's mostly energy itself—nonprotoplasmic. That's why it can fly too. A phaser blast affects it about like a stream from a fire hose would us: knocks it down, stuns it, but that's all. Now let's go look at Spock and I'll show you something else."

Spock was lying strapped down and under sedation, under the diagnostic panel.

"Watch the left indicator," McCoy said. "It's a dolorimeter—registers the level of pain. Right now it's preset at the maximum tolerance level. But if I open a channel to Spock . . ."

He moved a knob. At once, the indicator rose nearly to the top of the scale and froze there.

"That's what he's going through," McCoy said softly. "It's as though he were being consumed by fire, from the inside out. No wonder the poor devils go mad."

"And no wonder," Kirk said, "that they come to think killing each other is an act of mercy."

As he spoke, the indicator began to drop, very slowly. McCoy stared at it. "What the . . ."

Spock opened his eyes. "Hello, Doctor," he said weakly. "Hello, Captain."

"Mr. Spock! How do you feel?"

"Unwell. But these restraints will no longer be necessary. Nor will your sedations, Doctor. I will be able to return to duty."

"That's impossible," McCoy said.

"Spock, we've just seen what that pain can do to you," Kirk added.

"I regret my behavior," Spock said. "The pain greatly slowed my thinking. I did not even remember that we cannot set the ship down, on any planet. But I can control the pain now."

"How?" McCoy demanded.

"I am a Vulcan; we are trained to use our minds. Pain is only another kind of sensory input, which a trained mind ought to be able to handle."

"You're only half Vulcan," Kirk said. "What about the human half?"

"It is an inconvenience, but it is manageable. The creature—all of its thousands of parts—is pressing upon me even now. It wants this ship. But I can resist. It is not especially pleasant, but I assure you there will be no danger if you release me."

"The strongest mind in the world has to relax after a while," McCoy said. "If I put you on mild sedation . . ."

"No drugs, Doctor. My mind must be clear."

"Mr. Spock, I need you," Kirk said. "But I can't take

any chances. You stay here. Sweat it out for a while. If you can maintain control, then come back. Until then, do what the doctor says. That's an order."

Spock nodded. Then his face twitched and the dolorimeter shot up again. Closing his eyes, Spock whispered: "The mind rules. There is no pain. There . . . is . . . no . . . pain . . ."

On the bridge, Uhura had a call waiting from Starfleet. "*Enterprise* standing by, Commodore Anhalt," Kirk said.

"We've studied your reports of the situation on Deneva, Captain," Anhalt said. "We agree that the creatures, whatever they are, pose a clear and immediate threat to the area. It is our conclusion that, left alone, they would spread rapidly throughout that quadrant and perhaps farther. Can you tell us anything of the nature of the creatures?"

"Not yet. We're preparing to capture a specimen for analysis."

"Fine. But you are not on a specimen-collecting expedition, Captain. Regardless of the nature of the creatures, they must be destroyed—whatever the cost."

"Commodore," Kirk said, "there are more than a million innocent people on that planet. I may not be able to destroy the creatures without . . ."

"We are aware of that, Captain," Anhalt said evenly. "Your orders stand. We will expect your progress reports. Starfleet out."

The image faded. Kirk turned away from the screen to discover his first officer standing behind him.

"Spock, I gave you a direct order to stay in bed!"

"Until I was satisfied that I could maintain control," Spock said. "I am satisfied. So is Dr. McCoy."

"You're certain?"

"Absolutely."

"All right, then put your mind to work on this: How do I capture one of those creatures? They don't respond to the transporter any better than they do to phaser fire —and I'm not about to beam a man down there. I'd just beam back another casualty."

"Not necessarily," Spock said. "If the man's nervous

system were already inhabited, there would be little or nothing further the creatures could do to him."

Kirk stared at him. "I see what you're getting at," he said, "and I don't like it."

"Captain, in the same circumstances, I do not think you would hesitate for a moment. I simply claim the right to do as you would do, if our positions were reversed. I am the logical man for the job."

After a long silence, Kirk said: "It is so ordered. Be careful, and stay in constant touch with us."

"Of course, Captain."

Spock came back with two specimens—one of the creatures and a raving man. "I thought we would need somebody else who was already infected too," he said. "After all, the main problem is how to get the creature out of the body."

Aurelan reacted with shock and despair. "That is Kartan," she said. "We were to be married, before the creatures came."

She would not stay to watch McCoy testing, and Kirk could hardly blame her.

"It's the same picture, only more advanced," McCoy said. "In effect, he hardly has a nervous system of his own any more. The tissue has taken it over."

"It seems that at least we did find out what happened on Ingraham B and the other planets," Kirk said.

"No doubt about it. But what do we *do?*"

Spock came in, carrying the transparent case with the creature in it.

"Here it is," he said. "At first glance, a unicellular creature of sorts—but actually part of a creature. Its own level of activity is so low it doesn't even affect instruments. Its tremendous power is the result of participation in the whole. What it resembles more than anything else is a huge individual brain cell."

"How do you know?" McCoy said.

"You forget, Doctor, the creature has infiltrated my own system. I am in constant contact with it. I find it most annoying."

"I don't doubt that," Kirk said. "But how do we destroy it?"

"I think we have a clue. You will recall Noban, the

Denevan who flew into his sun. Just before his death, he cried out that he was free—that he had won. Apparently the proximity to the sun destroyed the creature controlling him."

"We already know they don't like light," Kirk said slowly. "But how do we expose them to light of that intensity? And what good would it do anyhow? A million of the creatures are inside human bodies."

"One was inside Noban's," Spock pointed out. "*Something* drove it out. But we need take no chances. The *Enterprise* has the capacity to turn Deneva into a miniature sun—a ball of nuclear energy. They would not survive that."

"Surely not," Kirk said thoughtfully.

"Now hold on," McCoy said. "Are you seriously considering this? Destroying a million people whose only crime was being victimized by these filthy things?"

"Our mission," Spock said somberly, "is to destroy the aliens—at whatever cost."

"Not at that cost! Jim, this idea is insane."

"These creatures are trying to spread out in the galaxy," Kirk said. "And the Denevans are already building ships for them. Aside from the fact that I have been given an order, we do not have much time."

"I have an alternative," Spock said.

"Great God, man," McCoy said, "spit it out!"

"Clearly any radiation intense enough to destroy the creatures would also destroy the people. But I think the hint we took from the fact that the creatures like shadows is a false lead. Light is a medium to them, like water is to a fish; they may simply prefer certain frequencies or levels, as some fish prefer saltwater to fresh. But consider this: If you have a free energy flow that for some reason you cannot conduct through a wire, a wave-guide or anything else of that sort, how do you direct it? Or, if you wish, disrupt it? The agency must be something that is both common and intense near a sun, yet completely harmless to human beings; remember, Noban's parasite was destroyed *before* he was."

"I'm no physicist," McCoy said. "Is there such an agency, or are we just playing games?"

"Certainly there is," Kirk exclaimed. "Magnetism!"

"That is what I had in mind," Spock said. "Of course,

we cannot generate a magnetic field as intense as a sun's, but it may not be necessary." He paused as Aurelan and Menen came in, explained his idea again quickly, and went on: "We have your son to thank for this, Menen. But what particularly interests me is that his parasite was not forced out gradually by the gradually increasing intensity of the general magnetic field. Instead, insofar as we can tell, it was wrenched out quite suddenly. This leads me to suspect that motion is the key—that what happened was that his ship passed through the rapidly whirling magnetic field of a sunspot. *That* is an effect we can duplicate. If I am right, it will pull the creature out like pulling a tooth."

"But probably a lot more painful," McCoy said. "Maybe even fatally so."

"It did not kill Menen's son. The heat did that. In any event, we have no course available but to try. Since I am already infected, the logical thing to do is to try it on me."

"And risk killing you?" Kirk said. "Things are bad enough already."

"Captain, the strain of maintaining my mental barriers is considerable. I do not know how long I can continue. When my guards go down—as inevitably they must—I will go insane. I would rather die by the hand of a friend. Furthermore, if I am insane, I am in a position to do the maximum possible amount of damage to the ship."

"Isn't there another question?" Aurelan said. "Mr. Spock is only half human. Even if the experiment is successful, it won't be conclusive."

"I have to work with what I have," McCoy said.

"You have Kartan," Aurelan said. "My fiancé."

They all looked at her in silence. When McCoy spoke, his voice was very gentle. "The risk," he said, "is extremely great."

"If you don't find a cure, he will die a raging maniac," she replied calmly. "Do you think I want that?"

McCoy glanced at Kirk, who nodded without hesitation.

"All right," McCoy said. "Thank you. I'll do my best."

It worked nicely. The creature emerged from all sides of Kartan's body at once, as though he were being enclosed in a balloon, and then was torn to shreds under the whirling electromagnets. He was still under sedation, but the dolorimeter promptly declined to normal level, and his face was peaceful for the first time since they had seen him.

"Congratulations, Mr. Spock," Kirk said. "And now I want you on that table, as fast as we can get Kartan moved out."

"No, sir."

"Why not? I should think you'd be eager to be rid of it! You volunteered before."

"True, Captain, but since then I have thought of something else. Do you realize that this leaves us just as badly off as we were before?"

Kirk frowned. Given the question, there was no need to explain it. There was absolutely no possibility of enveloping the whole of Deneva in such a field; Deneva's own natural field would fight it, and the *Enterprise* lacked the power to win such an invisible struggle. Nor was there anything like time to treat a million people individually.

McCoy obviously had also chased the chain of reasoning to its conclusion. "We are going to have to destroy the planet anyhow," he said harshly.

Aurelan straightened beside the sleeping Kartan. "Captain," she said. "They're my people. I grew up with them. I loved them. I've lost my brother. I don't want to lose anyone else. But I beg you, Captain, do what has to be done. Give the order."

"A million people . . ." Kirk said.

"Don't you understand?" Aurelan cried out. "There's no hope for them! Their brains are on fire! They want to die!"

Kirk stood as if frozen to the floor. "Brains on fire," he whispered. "Brains on fire. That's it. That's the answer!"

"Yes, Captain," Mr. Spock said. "That is my conclusion also."

"What is?" McCoy said. "You gentleman have lost me."

"It's like this," Kirk said rapidly. "Spock has already likened this—this composite organism to a gigantic brain. All the evidence we have points in the same direction. The individual cells are mindless, almost lifeless. It's possible, indeed it seems likely, that there is a central concentration of them somewhere. If we could kill that off . . ."

"I don't see that that follows at all," McCoy said. "The aggregate of the scattered cells could well be all there is to the brain, since we know the cells can communicate with each other. Why is it likely that there should be a concentration, too?"

"Because of the behavior of the creatures," Spock said. "They multiply uncontrollably until they overflow a planet. Not leave it—overflow it. The original central concentration is left behind. *Ergo,* it must still be there—wherever it is."

"And all we know about that is that it's somewhere in the Orion sector," Kirk said. "Mr. Spock, could the computer extrapolate the spread of these creatures backward, so to speak, and at least narrow down the possibilities to an area we'd have some hope of searching in time?"

"Of course," Spock said. "But you have something better, Captain."

"What's that?"

"You have me. That is why I do not want the treatment yet. I am infested; I am aware of the creature—not just the part of it that inhabits me, but the entire creature. As we approach the central concentration, I will know."

"Are you sure?"

For answer, Spock pointed. "It lies that way," he said. "I know that already, even though it must be fifty parsecs away."

"Posts!" Kirk shouted.

As they approached the critical Orion sector, it gradually became evident that not only was Spock aware of the nucleus of the creature—it was aware of him, and in some way realized that it must not allow this particular cell of itself to come closer. The pressure on Spock mounted unbearably. Though he still performed his duties, the sweat ran constantly down his face, which occasionally was twisted by a grimace that seemed to have no connection with anything he was doing or saying.

"Better let us extract that thing now," Kirk said. "We're zeroed in on the planet. There's no sense in your suffering any further."

"Sir, I would prefer to bear it just a little while longer. The final test of the theory is what happens to me—or does not happen—when that nucleus is destroyed. If the pain continues, we will know that we were wrong."

"Without prejudice to your own wishes or your will power, Mr. Spock, are you certain that there's no danger of your running amok again?"

"The danger exists," Spock said levelly. "However, I am fighting it. And I do not see how we can forfeit this test."

"I hate to say so," McCoy said, "but I think he's right, Jim."

"Very well," Kirk said. He looked at the main viewing screen, which was now showing the image of the target planet. It was utterly barren, though occasional faint geometrical patterns showed where there might once have been cities—before the creatures had come with their burden of agony and wiped them out. "It will be a pleasure to get rid of that monster. Arms Control, are those missiles primed?"

"Yes, sir," said a loudspeaker. "Two fully-armed planet-wreckers, programed and ready to go."

"Very well. Fire one."

A streak of light shot away from the *Enterprise*. For many long minutes nothing seemed to happen. Then the planet on the screen burst into a white blare of atomic fire. The screen backed hastily down the intensity spectrum.

At the same moment, Spock screamed. Two security men promptly grabbed him; Bones had been alert for just such an outcome.

"Stop! Stop!" Spock screamed. "My world—*my life*—"

"Fire two," Kirk said grimly. The planet was already breaking up, but he was taking no chances. Another colossal fusion explosion spread over the screen. When it had died away, there was nothing left to be seen but an enormous, expanding cloud of gas.

"So we have created a new Orion nebula," Kirk said. He turned to Spock. The first officer was standing quietly in the grip of the security man, while Bones hovered nearby with a hypo.

"Mr. Spock?"

Spock's eyes were glazed, and for a moment he seemed to have no mind at all. His face was blank, his mouth working. Then, gradually, life and sanity seemed to flow back into him.

"I am . . . recovering," he said formally. "The pain was . . . incredible . . . like nothing I had experienced before. For an instant I *was* that creature. I felt its death. But now . . . nothing."

"Now," McCoy said firmly, "we take you below and extract that thing from you. I will tolerate no further arguments on that score."

"No further arguments are necessary," Spock said. "Its purpose is served."

"Any word from Deneva, Lieutenant?"

"Rapidly getting back to normal, Captain," Uhura reported. "Menen says that the remaining creatures just wander about helplessly and seem to have almost no vitality left. To kill one, you need scarcely do more than stick it with a pin."

"Very good," Kirk said. "Mr. Spock, this may sound grandiose, but it's the truth. I think you have singlehandedly just saved the galaxy."

"No, sir, I think not."

"What could have stopped them if we hadn't?"

"Their own nature, Captain."

"Explain."

"A truly successful parasite," Spock said, "is commensal, living in amity with its host, or even giving it positive advantages—as, for instance, the protozoans who live in the digestive system of your termites and digest for them the wood that they eat. A parasite that regularly and inevitably kills its hosts cannot survive long, in the evolutionary sense, unless it multiplies with tremendous rapidity—much more rapidly than these creatures did. It is not pro-survival."

"In the evolutionary sense, maybe," Kirk said. "But evolution takes a long, long time. In the interim, you have at least saved millions of people from pain, madness and death."

"Believe me, Captain," Spock said, "I find that quite sufficient."

THE CITY ON THE EDGE OF FOREVER*
(Harlan Ellison)

Two drops of cordrazine can save a man's life. Ten drops of that unpredictable drug will sometimes kill. When a defective hypospray went off in McCoy's hand, a hundred times that amount was pumped into his body in a split second.

With a frenzied, incoherent cry, the ship's surgeon fled the bridge. Within minutes the entire ship was alerted. The library tapes on cordrazine said that at such dosages, paranoia was a frequent outcome—but McCoy knew the ship too well. By the time a search was organized, he had reached the transporter room and beamed himself down to the planet the *Enterprise* was orbiting.

The transporter had been monitoring what appeared to be a curious time disturbance on the surface of the unknown world. The settings had not been changed; whatever was down there, McCoy was now in the heart of it. Kirk would have liked to have had more information about it first, but there was no chance of that now. They had to go after McCoy. Kirk picked Spock, Scott, Uhura, Davis and a Security guard, and, of course, himself.

They materialized in the midst of extensive ancient ruins. Much of it was almost dust, but there were enough scattered sections of broken wall and piled stone to provide hiding places for McCoy.

This planet was *cold*. A burnt-out sun hung dolorously in the sky, producing a permanent, silvery twilight. It was a dead world, an ash. The ruins extended past the horizon—a city of tremendous size—but there could have

---

* The script for this story differed drastically in some respects from Mr. Ellison's original version, which he was kind enough to send to me. In writing this adaptation I tried to preserve what I thought were the best elements of *both* scripts; but it was tricky to manage and it is more than possible that I have wound up owing apologies all around. It was a poetic and brilliant piece to begin with; if it is a botch now, the fault is entirely mine.—JB

been no life in it for ten thousand centuries. It takes a long time for a sun to burn out.

In the midst of the desolation, one object was polished like new, drawing Kirk's eyes instantly. It was a large, octagonal mirror—or was it a mirror? Its framed, cloudy surface was nebulous, shifting. Whatever it was, it gleamed, untarnished, agelessly new. A cube, also untarnished but half-buried in dust and rubble, sat beside it. Spock aimed his tricorder at it.

"Whatever that is," Kirk said crisply, "make it the hub of our search pattern. Fan out."

The group separated quickly—all but Spock, who was drawing closer to the shining object, instead. He said, "Unbelievable!"

"Mr. Spock?"

"Sir, this one, single object is the source of all the time displacement we detected out in space. I do not understand where it gets the power, or how it applies it. It cannot be a machine, not in any sense that we understand the term, but . . ."

Kirk eyed the object. "Then what is it?"

At once, the dead air was stirred by a heavy hum; and then a resonant, vibrantly throbbing voice spoke from the object itself.

"A . . . question," the voice said. "A question. Since before your sun burned hot in space, and before your race was born, I have awaited a question."

"What are you?" Kirk said.

"I . . . am the Guardian of Forever."

"Are you a machine," Kirk said, "or a being?"

"I am both, and neither. I am my own beginning, my own ending."

Spock said, "I see no reason for answers to be couched in riddles."

"I answer all questions as simply as I can."

"What is your function, then?"

"I am a time portal. Through me the great race which once lived here went to another age."

"Past or future?" Spock said.

"The past," the voice said, like a sigh. "Always and only the past. And to their past, which you cannot share. I can only offer you yours. Behold—the birth of the planet you both share."

90

In the mirror, there was suddenly the image of a solar system forming out of a changing, cooling fireball . . . and somehow Kirk knew that it was not an image at all, but a distant view of a fact. A moment later, they were looking at a primeval, shoreless sea; and then, suddenly, a jungle of tree ferns.

"Mr. Spock," Kirk said thoughtfully, "if that is a doorway back through time, could we somehow take Bones back a day in time, then relive that accident? Stop that hypo spitting into him?"

"We would have to catch him first," Spock said. "Besides, Captain, look at the speed at which centuries are passing. To step through precisely on the day we wish would appear to be impossible."

"Guardian, can you change the speed at which yesterday passes?"

"I was made to offer the past in this manner," the Guardian said. "I cannot change."

Egypt waxed, waned, passed. Atlantis sank. Skin-clothed barbarians suddenly became Hellenes. Spock was getting it all into the tricorder.

"It's strangely compelling, isn't it?" Kirk said. "To step through there, lose oneself in another world—"

He was interrupted by a shout and a scrambling sound. He spun. McCoy, who evidently had been quite nearby, was headed straight for the time vortex at a dead run. Nobody but Kirk and Spock were anywhere near him.

Spock dropped the tricorder and intercepted, but McCoy, his eyes frighteningly wild, twisted away from him. That left no one but Kirk, who made a flying dive; but McCoy did a little dance step of broken field maneuvering and was free. Kirk landed painfully and rolled over.

"Bones!" he shouted. "No, no!"

But he was in time only to see McCoy disappear into the cloudy octagonal frame, his body popping out of sight as though it had been swallowed. Then the vortex was as blank as it had been when they first saw it.

"Where is he?" Kirk demanded.

"He has passed into what was," said the voice of the Guardian.

"Captain," said Uhura, a little breathlessly. She had arrived on the run. "I've lost contact with the ship. I was talking to them, and it suddenly went dead. No static; just . . . nothing."

"The communicator is all right?"

"Yes, sir. It just seems like there's nothing up there."

The Guardian said, "Your vessel, your beginning, all that you knew is gone."

Kirk felt a fearful sinking of his heart, remembering that episode when he and Spock and an archaic man named John Christopher had fought not to be noticed by the world of the 1970s. He said grayly, "McCoy has somehow changed history."

Scott had joined the party. He said, "This time we're stranded, Captain?"

Kirk did not answer, but Spock nodded. "With no past —no future."

"Captain," Uhura said. "I'm . . . I'm frightened."

Kirk looked slowly up into the black and star-littered sky of the nameless planet, empty now of the *Enterprise*, without even a sun to give it warmth and joy.

"Earth's not even out there," he said. "Not the one we knew. We are totally alone—without even a history."

"We shall have to remake it," Spock said.

"How, Mr. Spock?"

"We will have to go back in time ourselves—attempt to set right whatever it was that the doctor changed. I was recording images at the time he left. By synchronizing just out of phase with that, I believe I can approximate when to jump. Perhaps within a month before he arrived. Or a week if we are lucky."

"Guardian!" Kirk said. "If we are successful . . ."

"Then you will be returned. It will be as though none of you had gone."

"Just finding McCoy back there," Scott said, "would be a miracle."

Spock said, "There is no alternative."

"Scotty, when you think you've waited long enough— whatever 'long enough' might mean now—then . . ." Kirk shrugged. "Each of you will have to try it. Even if you fail, you'll be alive in some past world, somewhere."

"Stand ready, Captain," Spock said. "I think the time is coming around again."

They were standing in a seamy, down-at-the-heels city

street, with murky glass storefronts and an occasional square four-wheeled vehicle. Over one store was a large sign proclaiming:

CCC CAMPS—SIGN UP HERE

and beside it, another store with a sign that said FREE SOUP and a smaller sign with an arrow, reading FORM A LINE. Queues of shabby men in caps and shapeless coats were moving, very slowly, into both stores.

Spock said, bemused, "Is this the heritage my mother's people brag about?"

"This," Kirk said with disgust, "is what it took us five hundred years to crawl up from. Never mind that now—somebody's going to spot us pretty quickly, and our clothes aren't exactly period costumes. Let's do something about that first."

He drew Spock down the alley in which they had first popped into this world. "There's a line of clothes back there."

"I'm afraid I will draw attention either way, Captain."

"Well, Mr. Spock," Kirk said, "if we can't disguise you, we'll have to find a way to explain you. Here, put these on." He pulled down from a line two shirts, two pairs of pants, an old jacket and a wool stocking-cap.

"You might see if you can locate me a ring for my nose," Spock said. "But Captain, aside from the fact that this is theft, I do not believe we ought to change clothes out in the open. As I remember your history, old Earth was rather stuffy about such matters."

"That's right. Okay, let's march." Kirk rolled the clothing into a bundle and tucked it under his arm.

They made it back to the open street without incident. Kirk began to feel better. "You know," he said, "I rather like this century. Simpler, easier to manage. Why, I might even find I actually have a considerable talent for . . . *wump!*"

He had run squarely into the arms of a large, bulkily obvious Security-guard type. The blue-uniformed man looked them up and down, and then at the clothing bundle Kirk was shifting back and forth. At last he said pleasantly, "Well?"

"Uh, yes," Kirk said. "You are a police officer. I seem to remember . . ."

It seemed to be the wrong tack. Kirk let the sentence trail off and tried a friendly smile. The policeman smiled back, but he did not move. Behind Kirk, Spock said, "You were saying something about a considerable talent, sir?"

This was also a mistake, since it attracted the officer's attention to Spock, and especially to his pointed ears. Kirk said hurriedly, "My friend is, uh, Chinese, of course. The ears, ah, are actually easily explained. You see . . ."

The policeman remained absolutely silent. Kirk was stumped.

"Perhaps the unfortunate accident I had in childhood . . ." Spock prompted.

"In the fields, yes," Kirk said quickly. "Caught his head in a mechanical, uh, rice-picker. Fortunately . . . an Amellican missionary living nearby, who happened to have been a skilled plastic surgeon in civilian life . . ."

"Sure an' t'God that's enough, now," the policeman said. "Drop the bundle, hands up against that wall. Phwat a story."

"Yes, sir," Kirk said. As he was about to turn, he stopped and stared at the policeman's shoulder. "Uh, careless of your wife to let you go out that way."

"What?" the policeman said, raising his nightstick.

"Quite untidy, sir," Spock said, picking up the cue. "If you will allow me . . ."

He pinched the policeman's shoulder gently, and, equally gently, the policeman sagged to the pavement.

"And now, Captain . . ." he said.

"Yes," Kirk said. "As I recall, the appropriate expression is—flog it!"

Police whistles—an eerie, unfamiliar sound—were shrilling behind them as they ducked into an open cellar door. The cellar was dismal: a coal bin, an old furnace, mountains of litter, a few mildewed trunks, all looking like monsters in the dimness. They changed clothes quickly. Kirk wore the jacket; Spock pulled the stocking cap down over his elegant, dangerous ears.

Spock got out his tricorder. Nothing came out of it but

an unpleasant electronic squeal, like an echo of the fading police whistles.

The two men looked at each other over the coal pile. At last Kirk said, "Obviously this is not a game. Time we faced the unpleasant facts. Status, Mr. Spock?"

"First," Spock said precisely, "I *believe* we have about a week before Dr. McCoy arrives. But as far as being certain of that . . ."

"And arrives where? New York, Boise, Honolulu, Outer Mongolia?"

"Obviously, I do not know. There is a theory . . ." Spock hesitated. Then he shrugged and plowed on, "The theory is that time can be regarded as fluid, like a river, with currents, backwash, eddies. Like the solar-system analogies of atomic structure, it is more misleading than enlightening, but there may be a certain truth to it all the same."

"Mr. Spock, if I didn't know you better, I'd suspect you were trying to educate me."

"No, sir. I mean only to suggest that the same time current which swept McCoy to a certain place or event has taken us to the same place or event . . . Unless that is the case, I believe we have no hope."

"Odds?"

"Captain, in time there are no odds; you are pitting an infinite series of instants against an utterly improbable event. And yet . . ." Spock held up the tricorder. "Locked in here is the *exact* place, the exact moment, even exact images of what McCoy did back here. If I could hook this into the ship's computer for just a few moments . . ."

"Any chance that you could build a makeshift computer?"

"In this zinc-plated, vacuum-tube culture?" Spock said. "None at all. I have no tools, no parts, no supplies . . . I do not even know the line voltage."

"I see," Kirk said slowly. "Yes, it would pose a complex problem in logic. Forgive me, Mr. Spock. I do sometimes expect too much of you."

Spock's head turned sharply, but at the same time the overhead bulb in the basement went on yellowly and there was the sound of a door opening at the head of the stairs to the ground floor. A young woman's voice called strongly, "Who's there?"

Both men came to their feet as the girl came down the stairs. Despite the obvious savagery of the period, she seemed quite unafraid. She was simply dressed and not very pretty, but her voice was instantly arresting.

"We didn't want to trespass, miss," Kirk said. "But since it was getting cold out there . . ."

She looked at him with cool appraisal and said, "A lie is a bad way to say 'hello.' Was it really that cold?"

"Well," Kirk said, "no. We were being chased by a police officer."

"Because . . . ?"

"Petty theft. These clothes. We had no money."

"I see." She looked both of them over. "It's the same story all over. I need some help. Sweeping up, washing dishes, general cleanup. Are you willing to work?"

"At what scale of payment?" Spock said. Kirk looked at him in astonishment The first officer added, "I need radio tubes and so forth. Parts, wire . . . It is . . . a hobby."

"Fifteen cents an hour for ten hours a day," the girl said. "I'm not exactly wealthy, either. Will it do? Good. Your names?"

"I'm Jim Kirk. His name is Spock."

"I'm Edith Keeler," she said crisply, "and you can start by cleaning up down here."

She smiled pleasantly and went back up the stairs, leaving Kirk a little startled by her brisk, no-nonsense attitude and her utter fearlessness. At last he looked around, found a pair of brooms, and tossed one to Spock.

"Radio tubes and so on, eh?" he said. "Well, Mr. Spock, I approve. I think everyone should have a hobby. It keeps them off the streets."

The mission was a mixture of things which Kirk only vaguely recognized: part church, part dining room, part recreation area. It was furnished with tables and low benches, and there was a low dais at the front where workers dispensed soup and coffee. To one side, was a large tool box, fastened with an ungainly padlock with a dial on its face. Shabbily dressed men sat to either side of Kirk and Spock, waiting without enthusiasm. The nearest,

96

a small man with thin features who looked remarkably like some sort of rodent, eyed the two of them.

"You'll be sorry," he said, with exaggerated boredom.

"Why?" Kirk said.

"You expect to eat free or something? Now you gotta listen to Miss Goodie Twoshoes."

"Good evening," Edith's voice said, on cue. She was already striding toward the dais; now she mounted it. The meagerness of the audience did not seem to discourage her. She was both casual and cheerful. "Now, as I'm sure at least someone out there has said, you've got to pay for the soup."

There was some laughter. "Not that she's a bad-lookin' broad," the rodent said, *sotto voce*. "But if she really wanted to give a guy somethin' . . ."

"Shut up," Kirk said. Then, noticing Spock's eye on him, he added, "I'd like to hear this."

"Of course," Spock said, noncommittally.

"Let's start as we always do—by getting something straight," Edith said. "Why do I work, connive, and maybe even cheat a little in order to keep feeding you? I don't know. It's something that I do. But I've got no patience with parasites. If you can't break off with booze, or you've gotten out of the habit of work, or you *like* being a bad risk, I don't want you and you're not welcome to the soup."

Kirk listened with astonishment. He did not know what he had expected, but surely not this.

"Of course," she went on, "I know that every day is a fight to survive. That's all you have time for. But I've no use for a man who uses free soup as an excuse to give up fighting. To survive at all, you need more than soup. You need to know that your life is worth living, no matter what.

"Shadow and reality, my friends. That's the secret of getting through these bad times. Know what is, and what only seems to be. Hunger is real, and so is cold. But sadness is not.

"And it is the sadness that will ruin you—that will kill you. Sadness and hate. We all go to bed a little hungry every night, but it is possible to find peace in sleep, knowing you have lived another day, and hurt no one doing it."

"Bonner the Stochastic," Spock whispered.

"He won't be born for more than two hundred years. Listen."

"It's difficult not to hate a world that treats us all like this," Edith was saying. "I know that. Difficult, but not impossible. Somebody once said that hate is only the absence of love, but that's not a message that a man can absorb on an empty stomach. But there's something else that's true: Love is only the absence of hate. Empty the hatred from your hearts and you are ready for love. If you can go to bed tonight free of hatred, you have already won a major victory.

"And that's all of my sermon for today. Eat hearty, mates."

She stepped down and left the big, gloomy room.

"Most interesting," Spock said. "An uncommon insight."

"An uncommon woman," Kirk replied quietly; but Edith Keeler, coming up behind them, evidently overheard him.

"You two are uncommon workmen, Mr. Kirk," she said. "The basement looked like it had been scrubbed and polished."

Kirk thought about his days as a midshipman and at last saw some use for holystoning; but he said only, "Then we report back for more work?"

"At seven A.M. Do you have a flop for the night?"

"A what?"

Edith studied him curiously. "You're really new at this, aren't you? A 'flop' is a place to sleep. There's a vacant room where I live, two dollars a week. If you want it, I'll guide you there when we're through with these dishes."

"Indeed we do," Kirk said. "Thank you."

Like everything else, they had yet seen in this culture, the room was plain and depressing: a few pieces of scarred furniture, a sagging bed, limp and sooty curtains. Now, however, some of it was masked by the Medusa-head of wires, coils and banks of old vacuum tubes which Spock was attaching to his tricorder. As Kirk came in with a small paper sack of groceries, plus another small package of hardware, Spock said abstractedly, "Captain, I must have some sponge platinum, about a kilogram. Or a block of the pure metal, perhaps ten grams, would be even better."

Kirk shook his head. "I bring assorted vegetables for you, bologna and a hard roll for me. The other bag, I assure you, contains neither platinum, gold nor diamonds; nor is it likely to in the future. It has just a few second-hand pieces of equipment, and those took the other nine-tenths of our combined earnings for three days to fill your order for them."

"Captain, you're asking me to work with equipment which is hardly better than stone knives and bearskins."

"We have no choice," Kirk said. "McCoy may be here any day now. We've no guarantee that there's some current in time pulling us all together. This has to work—with or without platinum."

"Captain," Spock said glacially, "in three weeks at this rate, perhaps a month, I might complete the first mnemonic circuits . . ."

There was a knock, and then Edith poked her head through the door.

"If you can go out now," she said, "I can get you both five hours' work at twenty-two cents an hour. What on earth is *that*?"

"I am endeavoring, Ma'am," Spock said with dignity, "to construct a mnemonic circuit out of stone knives and bearskins."

"I don't know what that means," she said, "but if you want the work you'd better hurry." She withdrew.

"She's right. Let's go, Mr. Spock."

"Yes, Captain, in just a moment . . . It seems to me that I saw some tools for finely detailed work in the mission."

"Yes, the man who was working on the, uh, cuckoo-clock was using them. That girl has more things going on around there than a TKL computer. Clock repair project, woodworking, the tailor shop in the back . . ."

"You were quite right, Captain," Spock said. "She is a fascinating study. Well, I am ready now. I doubt that twenty-two cents an hour will advance me far, but those tools . . ."

"Just be sure you return them."

"Believe me, Captain," the Science Officer said, "my first taste of petty theft was also my last."

The auxiliary rig to the tricorder now nearly filled the room. It looked like a robot squid constructed by a small child, but it clicked, whirred and hummed purposefully. Clearly, Spock did not like the noise—he was used to machines that made as little fuss as possible—but he wasted no time trying to eliminate it. He straightened abruptly.

"Captain, I may have stumbled onto something."

Kirk sniffed. "You've got a connection burning somewhere, too."

"I am loading these lines too heavily. But this may be a focal point in time. Watch the tricorder screen. I have slowed the recording it made from the time vortex."

Kirk peered at the small tricorder screen. It showed Edith Keeler's face; then the image sharpened, and he realized that it was a newspaper photo. The paper was dated February 23, 1936—six years from "now." Over the photo was a headline: FDR CONFERS WITH SLUM AREA 'ANGEL'. The caption read, *The President and Edith Keeler today conferred for more than an hour on her proposal to . . .*

There was a mean snap of sparks, a curl of smoke and the image collapsed. "Quick!" Kirk said. "Can you get it back?"

"Even if I could, it would not help us," Spock said. "Something was wrong even before the short circuit. On the same memory trace, I saw a *1930* newspaper article."

"What of it? Either way, we know her future, Spock. Wit'in six years from now, she's going to become important nationally recognized . . ."

"No, sir," Spock said quietly. After a pause, he began again. "No, Captain.—What I saw was Edith Keeler's obituar. She never became famous. She will die this year in som kind of accident."

"You re mistaken! They can't both be true!"

"I'm afraid they can, Captain," Spock said. "She has two possible futures—depending upon what McCoy does."

"What . . . ? Oh, I see. McCoy has something to do with her living or dying. And in his present state . . ." The shock of the notion halted Kirk for an instant, but he forced himself to go on. "Mr. Spock, did McCoy kill her? Is *that* how all of history was changed?"

"I cannot tell, Captain. Something still worse is possible."

"What, man?"

"That he might have changed history by *preventing* her from being killed."

"Get this thing fixed! We've got to find the answer before McCoy gets here!"

"And what then, Captain?" Spock said. "Suppose we find that to set things right, Edith Keeler must die? That to restore our future, we must prevent McCoy from saving her? What then?"

"I don't know," Kirk said fiercely. "But we've got to find out. Did you get the jewelers' tools all right? That box was closed with a combination lock."

"Not a proper lock, sir. A childish device in probability . . ."

". . . and he opened it like a real pro," Edith's voice said behind them. Both men spun. She spared the jury-rigged apparatus only one glance, and then turned back to Spock. "Question: Why? I want to hear only one answer. Please make it the honest one."

Spock pointed to the rig. "You have seen this work going on before," he said. "I needed delicate tools. They would have been returned in the morning."

Edith eyed him. Perhaps his alien appearance gave her less than full confidence; or perhaps the very temper of the times was against him. She said, "Gadgetry doesn't impress me. Theft does. Out you go."

"Miss Keeler," Kirk said, "if Mr. Spock said they were important to have, and that you'd get them back in the morning, you may depend upon his word."

"I'll accept that," she said slowly, "on certain conditions. Chiefly, that Mr. Kirk answer my questions. And you needn't look so innocent, either. You know as well as I how out of place you both are here."

"Interesting," Spock said. "Where would you say we do belong, Miss Keeler?"

"You, Mr. Spock?" She nodded toward Kirk. "At his side. As if you've always been there, always will be. But where *he* belongs . . . well, I'll work it out eventually."

"I see," Spock said. "Well, I'll go on with this . . ."

"I'll go on with this—Captain," Edith Keeler said, smiling at Kirk. "Even when he doesn't say it, he does."

She led the way out. In the hall, she said, "By the way, why *does* he call you Captain? Were you in the war together?"

"We . . . served together."

"It shows. And you don't want to talk about it. Why? Is it something you think you've done wrong? Are you afraid of something? Whatever it is, let me help."

Kirk took her by the arms, and for a moment came very close to kissing her. He did not; but he did not release her, either.

" 'Let me help,' " he said. "A hundred years or so from now, I think it was, a famous novelist will write a classic using that theme. He recommends those three words even over 'I love you.' "

"Your tenses are rather mixed," she said. "A hundred years from now? And where was he? Or, where will he be from?"

"A silly question, a silly answer," Kirk said roughly. He pointed at the ceiling. "From about there. A planet circling that far left star in Orion's belt."

She looked up involuntarily; and this time, he did kiss her. He was not a little surprised to find it returned.

Spock turned as Kirk came back into the room. He asked no questions, but it was clear that he would welcome some answers.

"All she said was, 'Let me help you,' " Kirk said painfully. "She's something of a saint, Mr. Spock."

"She may be martyred," Spock said. "To history. Look here."

He switched on his apparatus. "This is how history went after McCoy changed it. I picked up the thread just after you went out. See: in the late 1930's a growing pacifist movement, called World Peaceways. Its influence on the government delayed the United States' entry into the Second World War. Apparently very few people knew that World Peaceways was German-controlled. While peace negotiations dragged on, Germany had time to complete its heavy water experiments."

"Hitler and Nazism won the war?"

"Yes. Because this lets them develop the fission bomb first. Let me rerun it, Captain. You will see that there is no mistake. And Edith Keeler was the guiding spirit of the peace movement."

"But," Kirk said, "she was *right*. Clearly, peace would have been . . ."

"She was right," Spock said, "but at the wrong moment. With the atomic bomb, and their primitive rockets to carry it, the Nazis captured the world, Captain. And after that, barbarism. The Nazi yoke was so heavy that the world tore itself apart trying to throw it off. Spaceflight never did develop."

"No," said Kirk, softly, in pain.

"And all that," Spock said implacably, "because McCoy came back and somehow kept her from dying as she should have, in a street accident. We have to stop him."

"Exactly how did she die? What day?"

"I can't be that precise," Spock said. "I am sorry, Captain."

"Mister Spock," Kirk said slowly, "I believe I am in love with Edith Keeler."

"I know," Spock said, very quietly indeed. "That is why I said, 'I'm sorry.' "

"And if I don't stop McCoy . . . ?"

"Then, you save her. And millions will die who did not die in what would have been our history."

"Abstract millions," Kirk said. "A different history. But Edith Keeler is here. She's real. She deserves to live."

"And so do Scott, Uhura, the others we left behind— or ahead. Sir, you are their Captain. They are waiting for you, in the ruined city on the edge of Forever. They, and the future that nurtured you. The choice is yours."

It had to be faced; but he could not face it—not yet. There would be time to decide when the crisis came. Of course.

In the meantime, there was still Edith . . . still. Spock said no more about the matter. He was with the two of them sometimes, somehow silently supportive. At others, guided perhaps by his peculiar form of semitelepathy, he vanished at just the appropriate moment.

This time, they emerged together from the mission, but separated almost at once. Spock started away from the twilight street, while Edith and Kirk crossed to the opposite sidewalk. Edith seemed even happier than usual.

"If we hurry," she said, "we can catch that Clark Gable movie at the Orpheum. I'd really love to see it, Jim."

Kirk smiled. "A what kind of movie?"

"That's funny," she said, looking up as if startled. "Dr. McCoy said almost the same . . ."

Kirk stopped dead in his tracks and whirled to face her, his heart suddenly racing.

"*McCoy?*" He took her by the shoulders, his fingers tightening until she winced. "*Leonard* McCoy? Edith, this is important."

"Why, yes. He's in the mission, in a little room upstairs. He's been very sick, almost raving, but I think he's nearly . . ."

"Spock!" Kirk shouted. "Edith—wait here for me."

He ran across the street, waving at the first officer. Spock turned back, his whole face a question; but he did not need to ask it. As the two men met in front of the mission door, McCoy came out of it.

The surgeon stopped dead in surprise, and then a grin split his face. There was a great deal of hand shaking and back thumping, with all three of them talking at once.

"Bones, where have you . . ."

"How'd you find me? And for that matter, where *are* we?"

"When Edith said 'Dr. McCoy' I . . ."

"Remarkable that you should have been that close to us . . ."

"I seem to have been sick for a long time . . ."

Kirk looked quickly back toward Edith. Her expression was mostly one of intense curiosity; but she also looked as though she felt a little left out of it all. As she saw him turn to her, she stepped out into the street.

She did not see the moving van lumbering down on her. *This was the time.* Without a moment's thought, Kirk ran toward her.

"Captain!" Spock's voice shouted. *"No!"*

Kirk froze, his body a solid mass of anguish. At the same time, McCoy's mouth opened in a wordless yell and he lunged for the curb. With a terrible flash of self-hatred, Kirk, knowing what *must* come next, threw himself in

McCoy's way, blindly, almost sobbing. McCoy stumbled. Edith cried out, and then there was the screaming shriek of brakes.

Then, silence.

"Jim," McCoy said raggedly. "You deliberately stopped me . . . Did you hear me? Do you know what you just did?"

Kirk could not reply. Spock took his arm gently. "He knows," he said. "Soon you will know, too. And what *was* . . . now *is* again."

Kirk sat at his desk in the *Enterprise,* back in uniform, staring at nothing. Behind him, Spock's voice said:

"Coordinates from the bridge, Captain."

The words meant nothing. The papers before him meant nothing. It was as though he were all but dead.

"Jim," Spock said.

The deadness did not lift, but a small thread of startlement crept through it. Kirk turned slowly.

"Mr. Spock," he said. "That's the first time you've ever called me anything but Captain."

"I had to reach you," Spock said gently. "But never mind the coordinates. Jim, on my world, the nights are very long. In the morning, there is the sound of silver birds against the sky. My people know there is always time enough for everything. You'll come with me for a rest. You'll feel comfortable there."

"All the time in the world . . ."

"And filled with tomorrows."

Suddenly, the bitterness welled up. "Not for her," Kirk said. "For us, but not for her. She was negligible."

"No, Captain, she was not. Her death saved uncountable billions of people. Both the living and the yet unborn. Far from negligible."

"And I failed her," Kirk said, groping for understanding. "I didn't save her. And I loved her."

"No. You acted," Spock said. "No woman was ever loved as much, Jim. Because no other woman was almost offered the universe for love."

It was only sheer luck that Marla McGivers was on the bridge when the SOS came in. Officially, Lieutenant McGivers was a controls systems specialist, but on the side, she was also a historian. Probably nobody else on board the *Enterprise* would have recognized Morse code at all, since it had gone out of use around the year 2000, in the general chaos following the Eugenics Wars; but she was a student of the period (though, Kirk thought, she looked a good deal more like a ballerina).

The SOS, when answered, changed promptly to the Morse for SS *Botany Bay*, and stayed there as if stuck regardless of further hails. Homing on the message, the *Enterprise* eventually found herself drawing alongside a dark hull of a ship of the CZ-100 class. The library computer said the last one of those had been built around 1994. Clearly a derelict, its signal left on automatic.

Except that the *Enterprise*'s sensors showed other equipment also still operating, over there across the vacuum between the two vessels. Other equipment—and heartbeats. They were very faint, but they seemed to be coming from some eighty or ninety sources. None were faster than four beats per minute. There were no signs of respiration.

"Aliens?" Kirk asked McCoy.

The surgeon shrugged. "You've got me, Jim. Even aliens have to breathe. Besides, the ship's name is in English."

"The English," Kirk said drily, "were notorious for not breathing, I suppose. Mr. Spock, can you trace the registry?"

"Nothing in the computer, Captain."

"Lieutenant McGivers, what can you tell us about the period when that ship was built?"

"Not as much as I'd like," Marla McGivers said. "The Eugenics Wars were caused by a group of ambitious scientists—of all nationalities—who were trying to im-

106

prove the race by selective breeding. They were pretty ⁕ ruthless about it, and before their identity was guessed, half the countries on Earth were accusing each other of being responsible for the plague of sports and monsters that was cropping up. The result was the last World War, and in the process, a lot of records were lost. I'm surprised that any ship from that era ever got off the ground."

"Well, we'd better go across and look it over," Kirk said. "Since you're a specialist in the period, you'd better be in the party. Scotty, I'll want you to inspect the machinery and see what's salvageable, if anything. Bones, you too."

"Why am I always included in these things?" McCoy complained. "I signed aboard to practice medicine, not to have my atoms scattered back and forth across space by a transporter."

"You're included because we hear heartbeats, and that is your department. Let's go."

It was almost dark inside the *Botany Bay*. Where the boarding party materialized, there was little to see but a long corridor, flanked on each side by row upon row of coffin-like drawers or canisters, each about two meters square on end, thrust into the wall. Each had a small green light blinking over it, producing eerie, confusing reflections. Kirk eyed them.

"Mr. Scott?"

"I don't make anything of it yet, sir. They look a little like food lockers—but why so many? Ah, there's a control panel."

"I've seen something like them," Marla said. "Or rather, drawings of them. They look like a twentieth-century life-support system."

McCoy applied his tricorder to the nearest cabinet. At the same moment, Scott said, "Ah, here we are!" and lights came on overhead. McCoy grunted with interest.

"Look here, Jim," he said. "A new reading. The lights seem to have triggered something inside."

Kirk did not have to look at the tricorder reading to see that. There was now a clear hum from the cabinet, and the little light had turned from green to red.

"I've got it!" Marla said suddenly. "It's a sleeper ship!"

This meant nothing to Kirk, but McCoy said: "Suspended animation?"

"Yes. They were necessary for long space trips until about the year 2018. They didn't have the warp drive until then, so even interplanetary travel took them years. We'll find crewmen in there, or passengers, sleeping, waiting for the end of their journey . . ."

"Or more likely, all dead," McCoy said. "On the other hand, those heartbeats . . . Is it possible, after all these centuries?"

Scott joined them, and in a moment had discovered that the front of the cabinet was actually a protective shield. Pulling this away, he revealed a transparent observation panel. On the other side, bathed in a gentle violet glow, was a motionless, naked man. He was extremely handsome, and magnificently built. His face reflected the sun-ripened Aryan blood of the northern Indian Sikhs, with just an additional suggestion of the oriental. Even in repose, his features suggested strength, intelligence, even arrogance.

"How beautiful," Marla said, as if to herself.

"This cabinet is wired to be triggered first," Scott said practically. "Maybe that means he's the leader."

"Or only a pilot," Spock added. "Or a doctor, to supervise the revival of the others."

"He's the leader," Marla said positively.

"Oh?" Kirk said. "What makes you think so?"

"Well . . . you can see it. A Sikh type. They were fantastic warriors."

"He *is* reviving," McCoy said. "Heartbeat up to fifty-two already, and definite breathing."

"Scotty, see if they're all like that."

The engineer went down the line, pulling off the shields and peering into each canister. "No sir," he said finally. "A mixed bag, Captain. Western, Mid-European, Near-Eastern, Latin, Oriental—the works. And all their lights are still green, as you can see yourself."

"A man from the twentieth century," Marla said, as if hypnotized. "Coming alive now. It's incredible!"

"It's about to be impossible," McCoy said, checking the tricorder again. "His heartbeat's beginning to drop back down. If you want to talk to this living fossil, Jim, I suggest we get him over to my sick bay right away quick."

108

"Oh no!" Marla said.

McCoy shot her a sidelong look, but he said, "I quite agree. A patient well worth fighting for. And think of the history locked up in that head!"

"Never mind the history," Kirk said. "It's a human life. Beam him over."

While McCoy worked on the sleeping man, Kirk took time out to collect more information from his officers.

"As near as I can work out their heading," said Spinelli, who had relieved Sulu at the helm, "they must have been trying for the Tau Ceti system."

"Makes sense. It's near Sol, and there are three habitable planets."

"Yes sir, but they would never have gotten there. Their port control jets took meteor damage, and the hits put them off course, too."

"Scotty, any log books or records?"

"Negative, Captain. They must have been in suspended animation when the ship took off."

"Ship's equipment?"

"Colonization gear mainly," the engineer said. "But quite heavy on armaments. I suppose that's typical of their era. Twelve of the life support systems malfunctioned, leaving seventy-two still operating. About a dozen of those are women."

"Seventy-two alive," Kirk said reflectively. "Any conclusions, Mr. Spock?"

"Very few, Captain. The CZ-100 class vessel was built for interplanetary travel only—*not* interstellar."

"They tried it."

"Granted," said the first officer. "But why?"

"Possibly because life on Earth had become so unbearable during the wars."

"Captain, consider the expense, just to begin with. Healthy, well-oriented young humans would think of some less costly way of surviving—or of committing suicide. It was ten thousand to one against their making it to Tau Ceti, and they must have known it. And another thing: Why no record of the attempt? Granted that the records are incomplete, but a maiden star voyage—the name *Botany Bay* should have been recorded a thousand times; one mention, at least, should have survived. But there is nothing."

"*Botany Bay*. Hmm. Lieutenant McGivers tells me that was a penal colony on the shores of Australia. Is that of some significance?"

"Are you suggesting a deportation vessel?" Spock said. "Again, logically insufficient. Your Earth was on the edge of another Dark Ages. Whole populations were being bombed out of existence. A group of criminals could have been eliminated in a far less expensive way than firing them off in what was the most advanced spaceship of its time."

"So much for my theory. I'm still waiting for yours."

"I do not have the facts, Captain. William of Occam said that one must not multiply guesses without sufficient reasons. I suggest that we take the *Botany Bay* to the nearest Star Base for a thorough study."

Kirk thought about it. "All right. Rig tractors for towing. In the meantime, I'm going to look at the patient."

In the sick bay, the man out of time was still unconscious, but now breathing regularly. Marla McGivers was standing to one side, watching.

"How is he, Bones?"

"By all rights he should be dead," McCoy said shortly.

"False modesty?"

"By no means. I'm good, but not *that* good. His heart stopped three times. When I got it going the third time, he woke up for a moment, smiled at me, and said 'How long?' I guessed a couple of centuries. He smiled again, fell asleep, and damned if his heart didn't stop a fourth time, and *start up again of its own accord*. There's something inside this man that refuses to accept death."

"He must have the constitution of an ox."

"That is not just a metaphor," McCoy said, pointing to the body function panel. "Look at that. Even in his present shape, his heart valve action has twice the power of yours or mine. Lung efficiency, fifty percent better. And courage! . . . Whoever he is, or whatever, it'll be a pleasure to meet him."

Kirk looked at Marla, and then said quietly to the surgeon, "I can get you agreement on that."

Apparently encouraged by the notice, Marla said, "Will he live?"

"If he gets some rest, he may," McCoy said tartly. "Beat it, both of you. This is a sick bay, not a wardroom."

Grinning, Kirk motioned Marla out and followed her. As she turned down the corridor, however, he said, "Lieutenant."

She stopped and turned. Kirk went on. "Lieutenant, if I were forced to rate your performance as a member of the boarding party today, I wouldn't give you a very high mark."

"I know, Captain," she said. "I'm sorry."

"That's not enough. At any one time, the safety of this entire vessel can rest upon the performance of a single crewman. The fact that you may find a strange man personally compelling is the worst possible excuse."

"Personally?" she said, flushing. "Captain, my second profession is history. To find a . . . a specimen from the past, alive . . . the sheer delight of anticipating what he might tell me . . ."

"More than that," Kirk said. "Men were much more adventurous then, bolder, more colorful."

She was silent for no more than a heartbeat. Then she said firmly, "Yes, sir, I think they were."

Kirk nodded. "That's better. If I can have honesty, I'll overlook mistakes—at least the first time. Dismissed."

As she left, Kirk turned to find McCoy watching him, smiling. "It's a pity," the surgeon said, "that you wasted your life on command, Jim. You'd have made a fair psychologist."

"Thanks, Bones. but command is better. It covers every other subject."

"Touché—or should I say, checkmate?"

It was only a few hours later that McCoy called Kirk on the bridge. "Captain," he said, "I have a patient with questions—and I don't mind telling you, patients like this could put medicine out of business. Can you come down?"

The big man from the *Botany Bay*, now dressed in a tunic from the stores of the *Enterprise*, was still on his bed; but he was indeed awake—vitally awake. Kirk introduced himself.

"Thank you," the man said. "I am told I have slept for

111

two centuries or more, and am on board a real starship —not a makeshift like mine. What is our heading?"

Kirk was both amused and annoyed. "Would you care to give your name first?"

"No, I would not. I have a responsibility. If you are indeed a commander, you will recognize it. Where are we going?"

Kirk decided to yield for the moment; there was no point in insisting on a contest with a man just yanked back from the edge of death, no matter how arrogant he was. "Our heading is Star Base Twelve, our command base in this sector."

"Which is?"

"I doubt that identifying the sector would do you any good. It is many parsecs beyond the system you were headed for, and our galactic coordinate system probably doesn't correspond with the one you're used to."

"Galactic," the man said. "I see. And my people?"

"Seventy-two of the canisters are still functioning. The people will be revived when we reach Star Base Twelve. We wanted to see how we fared with reviving you, first."

"Logical and hard-headed; I approve. I do begin to grow fatigued. Can we continue the questioning at another time?"

"You haven't answered any questions yet," Kirk said, "except by inference."

"I apologize," the big man said at once. "My name is Kahn. I command the *Botany Bay* Colonizing Expedition. I think perhaps I could answer your questions better if I knew your period, your terminology and so on—perhaps something to read during my convalescence would serve. History, technology, whatever is available."

It seemed a sensible request. "Dr. McCoy will show you how to hook your viewing screen here into our library tapes. And I think Lieutenant McGivers would enjoy filling you in on the history."

"Very good." Kahn smiled. "I have two hundred years of catching up to do. I . . ."

Suddenly, his eyes closed. McCoy looked at the body function panel.

"Asleep," McCoy said. "Well, I'm glad he's got *some* human weaknesses."

It was not until Kirk was on his way back to the bridge

that he fully realized how little Kahn had told him. Irritated, mostly at himself, he collared Spock at the computer. "Anything?"

"Nothing about a star flight until the Alpha Centauri expedition of 2018," the first officer said. "How is the patient?"

"Arrogant—and clever. Enormously powerful. And with enormous magnetism. Not at all what I expected in a twentieth-century man."

"Interesting. Possibly a product of selective breeding."

"That had occurred to me," Kirk admitted. "If I wanted a superman, he's very much the kind of outcome I'd shoot for."

"Exactly, Captain. He is almost a stereotype of an Earthman's dreams of power and potency. And from what I can put together from the fragments of the record, just the kind of man who precipitated the chaos of the 1990s."

"Oh? I thought it was a group of scientists."

"Partly true," Spock said, "and partly, I would judge, a comfortable fiction. The scientists encouraged carefully arranged marriages *among themselves,* and applied their knowledge of heredity to their *own* offspring. The sports and monsters did not appear until after the war was well started, and almost surely were spontaneous mutations erupting from all the ambient radioactivity. The scientists stayed aloof and went right on breeding what they thought was *Homo superior.*"

"Fact?" Kirk demanded. "Or just that old legend of the mad scientists again?"

"Mostly deduction," Spock said. "But the scientists existed. Not mad—not raving mad, anyhow. Dedicated men who believed their wards would grow up to seize power peaceably, put an end to war, famine, greed—a noble ambition, which of course misfired."

"And our patient?"

"One of those children. His age would be right. A group of aggressive, arrogant young men *did* seize power simultaneously in over forty nations. But they had overextended themselves; they could not hold what they seized. That much is fact. And one more thing, Captain. Are you aware that some eighty or ninety of those people were never brought to trial, were never even found after the chaos? No bodies, no graves, no traces?"

"I certainly wasn't," Kirk said.

"And they should have been found, or the authorities should have pretended that they had been found. Think of the panic among the remaining, starving war-weary people even to suspect that eighty Napoleons might still be alive. And, Captain . . ."

"Yes," Kirk said heavily. "I'm no match for you as a logician, Mr. Spock, but even I can see where that sentence is leading. You think those eighty Napoleons are *still* alive—and we have seventy-nine of them in tow, and one on board."

"Precisely, Captain."

Kirk thought about it for quite a while.

"It stands up," he said. "But what we're left with, is that we can get no more pertinent information anywhere except from Kahn himself. He's got a mind like a tantalum-lined vault, so we'll never force it out of him. We'll have to try to charm it . . . which probably won't work either. Maybe we can use the customs of his own time to disarm him. I'll see what Lieutenant McGivers has to suggest."

What Marla McGivers had to suggest was a formal dinner, attended by all the major officers of the *Enterprise*, as a welcome for Commander Kahn to the twenty-third century. She was obviously far from disinterested in the proposal, and Kirk suspected that Kahn had already made his first new conquest in the new century; but there were no regulations against romance, and in any event, Kirk had nothing better to suggest.

Marla appeared with a new and totally anachronistic hair style which went a long way toward confirming Kirk's suspicions. As for Kahn, it was impossible to tell whether or not he was charmed; he far too efficiently charmed everybody else, instead. There seemed to be no situation in which he could not feel at home, after only a few minutes' appraisal.

Then, over the brandy, it suddenly turned out at least one officer of the *Enterprise* was not prepared to recognize charm even if he were hit over the head with it. Spock said, "But you still have not told us why you decided on star travel, Commander Kahn—nor how you managed to keep it out of the records."

"Adventure, Mr. Spock. There was little else left to be accomplished on Earth."

"There was the overthrow of the Eugenics tyrannies," Spock said. "Many men considered that a worthwhile effort."

"A waste of spirit in a desert of shame," Kahn said. "There was much that was noble about the Eugenics crusade. It was the last grand attempt to unify humanity, at least in my time."

"Like a team of horses under one harness, one whip?"

"I refuse to take offense, Mr. Spock," Kahn said genially. "Much can be accomplished by a team. It was a time of great dreams—great aspirations."

"Great aspirations under petty dictatorships? Never in previous history, at least."

"I disagree," Kahn said. "One man, not many, would eventually have ruled. As in Rome under Augustus—and see what that accomplished—Captain Kirk, you understand me well. You let your second-in-command attack me, and through me, you; yet you remain silent, and watch for weakness. A sound principle."

"You have a tendency," Kirk said, "to express your ideas in military terms, Commander Kahn. This is a social occasion."

"It has been said," Kahn said easily, "that social occasions are only warfare concealed. Many prefer their warfare more honest and open."

"There was open warfare on Earth," Kirk said. "Yet it appears that you fled it."

"Not much can be done with a nearly destroyed world."

"In short," Spock said, "you were afraid."

Kahn's eyes flashed. "I have never been afraid."

"And that does not frighten you?"

"How? I don't understand you, Mr. Spock. How can a man be afraid of never being afraid? It is a contradiction in terms."

"Not at all," the first officer said. "It is a null class in the class of all classes not members of the given class."

Kahn was now beginning to look angry. Kirk, secretly a little amused, interposed. "I'm sorry, Commander, but you just pushed Mr. Spock's logic button, which has a tendency to make him incomprehensible for the next ten minutes or so. Nevertheless, I think his question a good one. You say you have never been afraid; yet you left at the very time mankind most needed courage."

"Courage! How can one impart courage to sheep? I offered the world order. *Order!* And what happened? They panicked. I left behind nothing worth saving."

"Then," Spock said, "do you imagine that this ship, to take a simple example, was built by sheep, out of panic? I do not further impugn your logic, Commander Kahn, but I am beginning to mistrust your eyesight."

Marla, who had been completely silent since the start of the discussion, stood up so suddenly that coffee slopped in saucers all the way around the table.

"I never thought," she said in a trembling voice, "that I'd ever see so much rudeness to a starship guest."

"Was *I* rude?" Spock said mildly, raising his eyebrows. "If so, I apologize."

"And I," said Kirk, repressing another grin.

"I quite accept your apologies," Kahn said, also rising. "But if you will excuse me, gentlemen and ladies, I am tired. It has been a good many centuries, and I would like to return to my quarters. If you would guide me back, Marla . . . ?"

They went out, followed, at a slight motion of the head from Kirk, by every other guest but Spock. When the room was empty, Kirk said, "And McCoy calls *me* a fair psychologist! I've never seen a better needling job in my life, Mr. Spock."

"I myself am not very happy with it, Captain," the first officer said. "The human half of my make-up seems to go to sleep just when I need it most. Consider, really, how little we have learned. The man's name: Sibahl Khan Noonien. From 1992 through 1996, military chieftain of a quarter of your world from South Asia through the Middle East, and the last of the tyrants to be overthrown. And apparently very much admired, as such men go; there was very little freedom under his rule, but also there were no massacres, and no war until he was attacked by a lesser dictator of his own breed. A man of power, who understands the uses of power, and who *should* have been much admired by the people whom he calls sheep, the people who feel more comfortable being led."

116

"And you got all that just from what he said tonight? I would say that's considerable."

"It is not what we need to know," Spock insisted. "The main question is, why did he run away? *That* was what I was hoping to elicit from him. But he caught me at it. I do not call that very good psychology."

"I see what you mean," Kirk said reflectively. "Until we know that, we can't know what he might intend now —or what risks we might run in reviving the other seventy or so of them. We will just have to try another gambit . . . But there's one other thing. What was the point of that question about being afraid of never having been afraid? I thought for a moment that I saw what you were driving at, and then you lost me in your logical technicalities. Isn't the question what you would call a tautology?"

"No, Captain," Spock said. "But I was trying to make it look like one. I was not trying to confuse you, certainly, but Commander Kahn—and I hope that at least there, I succeeded. Fear is an essential reaction to the survival of any sentient creature. If he does not know fear, he never knows when it is sensible to run; and yet, Commander Kahn ran. Since he claims never to have felt fear, what other reason can he have had?"

"Hmm," Kirk said. "I've never seen a single sentient creature that didn't feel fear when it was appropriate. Yet he was very convincing on that very point."

"Indeed he was," Spock said. "And, Captain—that *scares* me."

Nothing Spock had ever said before had quite so stunned Kirk. As he stared at his Science Officer, the vacated, somehow sadly messy scene of the formal dinner suddenly rang with the alarm to General Quarters.

"Abrams in Security, Captain. Kahn's missing."

"McCoy here. Kahn's not here. No sign of McGivers, either—not even in her quarters. And he's not there."

"Transporter room here. We've had a guard slugged, Lieutenant Adamski is missing, and there's been a lot of power expended in the last half hour."

"Scott reporting. I . . ."

"Uhura, what happened to Scotty? Get him back!"

"Dead channel, Captain. I can't raise the arsenal, either."

117

"Spock, send somebody down."

"All turbo elevators inoperative. Emergency exits jammed."

The lights began to go down. "Batteries!"

"Shunted out, Captain. Also, the atmosphere's off."

"Engineering! Scott! What's going on down there? Scotty!"

And then they heard Kahn's voice. It was coming through Uhura's own board, though it was impossible to imagine how Kahn had made the crippled array speak.

"He's not able to talk with you at the moment, Captain," Kahn said. "I'm afraid your ship is mine—or rather, ours. I have almost all my people aboard her, at every key point. Everything is jammed; you have perhaps ten minutes before you suffocate. Would you like to negotiate with me?"

"Uhura, can you raise Star Ship Command?"

"No, sir, this board is a dead duck. I can't even dump a message capsule."

"Brilliant," Spock said softly.

There was only one thing left to do. "Security Five, Mr. Spock. Flood all decks."

"Bypassed, Captain. Commander Kahn seems to have been a very quick student."

"Can we go to Six?" That would fill the air with radioactive gas from the fusion chamber and kill almost everyone on board; but . . .

"No sir, we cannot. Nothing is left but Destruct. That's still alive."

"The air up there should be getting quite toxic by now," Kahn's voice said. "You don't have much time."

"What do you want, Kahn?"

"Surrender of the bridge."

"Refused," Kirk said.

"Very well. It is academic, anyhow. In ten minutes, every person on the bridge will be dead."

Nothing further was heard from Kahn after that. Slowly, the air turned foul. After a while, nobody was conscious but Kirk, and then . . . and then . . .

Kirk awoke, with considerable surprise, in the briefing room. His entire staff seemed to be with him—all weak, but all alive. They were heavily under guard by Kahn and a group of men very like him, all carrying *Enterprise* phasers. The men from the *Botany Bay* were inarguably splendid-looking specimens—large, strong, healthy, handsome, and above all, alert.

"Very good," Kahn said. "Now we can talk. You see, Captain, nothing changes—except man. Your technical accomplishments are illusions, simply the tools which men use. The key has always been man himself. Improve a mechanical device and you double your capacity; improve man, and you gain a thousand fold. You, I judge, are such a man, Captain, as am I. You would be wise to join me."

Kirk said nothing. Kahn turned to Spock. "I am tempted," Spock said. "I admire your tactics . . . but not, I am afraid, your philosophy. And I know from history how self-appointed supermen treat mixed breeds. Let us see how you run the ship by yourself."

"You will see. My offer to you is closed. Navigator, I want you to set course for the nearest colonized planet—one with port facilities and a population which is not afraid of discipline."

"Go to blazes," Spinelli said.

"It is as I thought," Spock said. "You may know the *Enterprise* well, Commander, but your newly revived colleagues do not. I think we have a stalemate."

"Do we? Dr. McCoy, you maintain a decompression chamber in your laboratory, isn't that so? Yes, I know it is. Joaquin, take Captain Kirk to the chamber. Put him inside, and lower the pressure to zero. I trust the rest of you understand what that means. You can spare him that. All I want from you is your word that you will continue performing your duties."

"Nobody," Kirk said harshly, "is to lift a finger to save me. I so order."

"I am not bluffing," Kahn said pleasantly. "If, of course, you allow your Captain to die, you will all follow him, one by one, into the chamber."

Kirk caught Marla's eye. She was staring wide-eyed at Kahn. Evidently she had discovered something she hadn't taken into account.

There was a blare from a wall speaker, and then a babble of angry, excited crowd noises. "Kahn," said an unfamiliar voice, "this is Paul in the recreation room.

119

They're getting out of hand. I may have to kill a few of them."

"Do so, then."

"No!" Marla said. "I have friends there . . . Kahn, please. If I could talk to them . . . reassure them . . . There's no need to kill them."

"You may attempt it," Kahn said. "Be certain they understand that I have no compunctions about killing if I'm forced to."

The guards hustled Kirk out, with Marla in tow. Perhaps they were unfamiliar with the ship in detail, but they certainly knew their way to McCoy's laboratory. They bundled Kirk into the decompression chamber as though they were doing nothing more interesting than autoclaving a rack of test tubes. The door shut, and a moment later Kirk heard the pumps begin to throb.

For some reason, he felt neither alarmed nor resigned. His chief emotion was anger, at being put through asphyxiation twice in one hour.

There seemed to be nothing to do about it, however.

Then the door hissed and swung back. Kirk stepped out cautiously. One of the supermen, the one called Joaquin, was out cold on the floor, with Marla standing over him, a wrench held awkwardly in her hands. The other guard evidently had gone off somewhere.

"Are you all right?" Marla said tremulously.

"I think so. The pressure didn't have time to drop much. I'm glad to see you're good for something." He stooped and picked up Joaquin's phaser.

Marla grasped his arm. "Captain, please," she said.

"Well?"

"I saved your life. Promise me you . . . won't kill him."

"No promises," Kirk said, looking around the laboratory. After a moment, he spotted what he wanted; a bulb of the anesthetic gas McCoy used to capture specimens. He juggled it with pleasure. "Stay here and try not to get yourself any deeper into trouble than you are. I think I am about to bag myself some choice items for some zoo."

It was not all that easy. Before it was over, one of the supermen was dead, and almost everyone else on both sides was considerably banged up. At last, however, the survivors from the *Botany Bay* were locked in a hold, and Kirk and his officers reassembled in the briefing room.

"Well, Mr. Spock," Kirk said, "I think we know now why they left the Earth."

"Yes, sir. To free themselves of the rabble, and start fresh. In my opinion they would never have succeeded, even had they made it to a habitable world. The man who cannot know fear is gravely handicapped."

"We are about to put that to the test. Have Kahn brought in here, please."

Kahn was brought in, under guard, with Marla behind him. Both looked at Kirk defiantly.

"At present," Kirk said, "we are orbiting a planet in a system unknown to you, and which I shall not further identify. It is savage and inhospitable, but with breathable atmosphere and land which can be cultivated. You have the following choice: To be put ashore on this world, with a minimum of survival equipment; or, to be taken to Star Base Twelve to be assigned to rehabilitation. The second choice would be rather drastic in your case, but it would enable you to fit into our society. Which do you prefer?"

"Captain," Kahn said, "I suppose you will remember that Lucifer said when he fell into the pit."

"I remember it well. I take it that's your answer?"

"It is."

"It may interest you to know that Systems Officer McGivers, given the choice of standing court martial or sharing your exile, has chosen to go with you."

Kahn looked at her and smiled. "I knew I was right about you," he said. "You have the fire. And think of this: we have what we wanted after all—a world to win." He swung on Kirk. "And, Captain, we will make it an empire. You'll see."

"If you do," Kirk said, "you'll have earned it. Guards, beam them down."

Kahn exited without a backward look, but Marla turned at the door.

"Goodbye, Captain," she said. "I'm sorry. But I do love him."

"I wish you luck, Lieutenant."

After a short silence, Scott said, "It's a shame for a

121

good Scotsman to admit it, but I'm not up on my Milton. What *did* Lucifer say after he fell into the pit?"

"He said, 'Better to reign in hell than serve in heaven.' Mr. Spock, clear for space. I want to get under way as soon as possible."

"Yes, Captain. What shall I do with the *Botany Bay?*"

"Hmm . . . You'd better dump it into—no, on second thought, let's keep it in tow. I suppose there are still things aboard her that the historians will want to see. At the moment, though, whenever I say 'historian' I have to repress a shudder."

"Let us think ahead, then," Spock said. "It would be interesting to come back to this system in a hundred years and see what crop had sprung up from the seed we have planted today."

"It would indeed," Kirk said. "But I'll tell you something else, Mr. Spock. I only hope that in a hundred years, that crop won't have sprung right out of the ground and come out looking for *us.*"